SOUTHERN STORIES

SOUTHERN STORIES

THE FAMILY SECRET

ALBE CHARLES

Charleston, SC
www.PalmettoPublishing.com

Southern Stories
Copyright © 2022 by Albe Charles

First Edition

Hardcover: 978-1-68515-210-9
Paperback: 978-1-68515-211-6
eBook: 978-1-68515-212-3

DEDICATION

This book is dedicated first to God, the great Creator, who through the power of words brought all of creation into existence, saying "Let there be." It is dedicated to my dad, Albert, who told me that I was born to succeed, and my mom, Charlena, who told me not to hide my light or downplay the gifts the Lord gave me. They, along with my maternal grandparents, Otto and Ethel; my paternal grandparents, William and Tealie; and my adopted grandmother, Ruby, sleep with the ancestors. This book is dedicated to my Uncle Hayward, who represents my paternal family. His examples of success and dignity have always been a source of inspiration. It's dedicated to my Aunt Peggie, who represents my maternal family. She is the epitome of what an aunt should be. She has supported every part of my life since the day I entered this world. To my sister, Trina, who has fulfilled every role I have ever needed throughout my life: sister, mom, friend, counselor, caretaker, cheerleader, and confidant. This book is dedicated to my entire village, every sibling, cousin, family member and friend who has made my life better just by being in it. Mine is a village rich in faith, history, love, and laughter. This book is dedicated to all the authors whose works have educated, entertained, or inspired me. Last, this book is dedicated to all the storytellers whose words will never be seen in print.

THANK YOU

Writing this book has been a 20-plus year journey with many stops and starts, mostly due to procrastination. I am very grateful to the Lord for His grace and kindness. I am appreciative to every person who prayed, encouraged and cheered me on to the finish line. Thank you to Trina, Aunt Peggie, Veronica and Jackie for being a sounding board; thank you to Lawrence, my best friend, who supported me from the moment the first page was written so many years ago; and thank you to my literary angels, the men and women who generously offered their time, wise counsel and professional insight. Every ounce of input and assistance was received with sincere gratitude. Finally, thank **you** for taking time to read *Southern Stories: The Family Secret.*

PREFACE

A healthy imagination exceeds the limits of time and space. And it can give life to the loved ones we've lost. As a child I was always fascinated by listening to "grown folks talk." I heard stories about people, places, and situations that I had neither all the information about nor fully understood, so my imagination filled in the gaps. In my mind I could travel and meet these interesting people engaged in all sorts of drama and adventure.

When I began to read the works of authors like James Baldwin, Maya Angelou, Richard Wright, J. California Cooper and Bebe Moore Campbell, I connected to their characters and settings because they reminded me of the types of people and places I had heard about so many times before.

My book, *Southern Stories: The Family Secret*, is an ode to all these stories— real and fiction —that have taken me on so many journeys throughout my life. It is also a celebration of my southern roots. Sadly, this book is easily relatable because secrets are an unfortunate dynamic within far too many families.

Set in the 1970s in the Deep South of Simpson County, Mississippi, this is a fictional story of the Smith family, a strong, close knit family led by parents Charlie and E. May. Both are hardworking, respected members of the community. Charlie is a businessman who can fix anything. He has a reputation for being straightforward and reliable. He doesn't talk without purpose, and while not violent or aggressive, he is not afraid of confrontation. E. May is a woman of faith who makes a living working as a domestic and selling her baked goods. She and Charlie have been married for over thirty years. They grew up as friends in the same little town of Pinola. Charlie knew from elementary school that he would one day marry E. May, even though she told him repeatedly throughout their teen years she was not interested. She changed her tune, however, during their senior year in high school when she let Charlie take her to the prom. They danced and laughed all evening and were together from that moment on. They have four children: Johnny, Freddy, Cassie, and Emma. All of them were raised with a strong sense of love and respect for God, family and others.

When older sister Cassie's husband has an affair with her sister, Emma, the family's commitment to those values is compromised by the concern for public perception. The act of infidelity and an unplanned pregnancy give life to betrayal, lies, and secrecy, unraveling the fabric of this once tightly woven family and sending Cassie fleeing to the city of Jackson. There she meets a mysterious man who awakens her romantically. Her concerns about his criminal activity are not enough to deter her from getting involved, and she soon trades one set of moral concerns for another. This family's drama is a cautionary tale about how lies, though not seen or known, can have very real and entangling consequences.

PART I

CHAPTER ONE

Happy Birthday Baby Lena!

Baby Lena stood on the dinette chair amid the smiling well-wishers, looking from face to face. Most of her family was together for her seventh birthday. She hadn't seen her Grandpa Charlie, Grandma E. May, Uncle Johnny, Uncle Freddy, and Aunt Emma look this happy in a long time. In fact, the last time they were together, Aunt Emma cussed out everybody in the family. Baby Lena, as they called her, hoped that didn't happen today. But if Uncle Johnny brought out that brown sack he always carried and he and Aunt Emma started to drink, it was definitely a possibility.

"Make a wish Baby Lena!" said Helene, her favorite cousin. She could hardly see Helene standing among all the adults.

"That's right, girl. Make a wish and blow out them candles, so we can cut that cake," said Grandpa Charlie.

Baby Lena shut her eyes and took a deep breath. She wanted to wish for her mommy and daddy to be there with her, but she didn't believe seven candles were enough for such a big request. *Maybe if I was turning ten*, she thought to herself. Instead, she wished she could see either her mommy or daddy before her next birthday.

As Baby Lena blew out the candles, there was a hard knock on the front door. "Who is it?" Grandpa Charlie yelled in irritation.

"It's me, Ray! Open up! I wanna say 'Happy Birthday' to my baby girl!"

"What that fool doin' here?" said Emma under her breath but loudly enough to be heard.

"He probably drunk or in trouble," said Freddy.

"Or he drunk *and* in trouble." Emma rolled her eyes in disgust.

Despite how the family felt, Baby Lena was excited that her father had come to see her on her birthday. She had no way of knowing that her very existence was at the heart of their strained encounters with him. Ray was well known around town. He was a good-looking man with deep, slanty brown eyes and a smile that always displayed the gap between his two front teeth. He wasn't a tall man, but his personality was larger than life. Grandma E. May often said, "That boy could charm the pants off a snake."

Baby Lena was a daddy's girl. She would often gaze at herself in the mirror, admiring how much she looked like him. It was true she had her father's round face and honey-colored skin, but she also had her mother's big brown eyes and soft black hair.

Bam, bam, bam. "Y'all gon' let me in? I wanna see Baby Lena!" said Ray.

"Charlie, let the boy in," said Grandma E. May.

Forced by his wife's words, Charlie got up and headed to the front door. "Alright, but I ain't for no foolishness. Not today. We tryna' enjoy this baby birthday as a family, and here he come."

"He *is* family, and I don't wanna hear another word," said E. May, glaring at Emma.

"Hey family! Ma E. May, how's my favorite girl?" shouted Ray, throwing up his hand to acknowledge the rest of the family. He made his way to the tall and stately lady to take her and dance her around a few times before turning his attention to Baby Lena.

"There she is! The birthday girl! Give your daddy a big hug," he said, taking notice of his daughter still standing in the chair. "Your daddy came a long way to see you," he said lifting her and peppering her face with kisses.

Baby Lena closed her eyes and clasped her hands around her father's neck as he hugged her. She thought to herself, *Part of my birthday wish has already come true. Now all I need is my mommy to come home.*

———

"Cassie, wake up!"

"What?!" said the woman, shifting from one side to the other on an old, worn couch. "Kat, I'm not sleep."

"Like hell you ain't. You've been there since three o'clock this morning, and it's four o'clock in the afternoon."

"Well, I'm not sleep *now*," she said sitting up.

Trying to regain her focus, she scanned the storage room with its faded wallpaper and neatly stacked boxes. When she realized she was still in her clothes from the night before, Cassie used her hands to try to press out the wrinkles in her paisley printed, kimono-style dress.

She was an attractive woman with a small waist and curvy hips. Though short, she had shapely, athletic-looking legs that were a family trademark. Unlike Ray's honey-colored complexion, she had a lighter skin tone. And she didn't have what people call "good hair." Hers was long wavy, and soft, and she kept it combed in either an updo or low bun style. Cassie was educated and didn't talk much until she drank, and she hadn't started drinking until she arrived in Jackson three years ago. She had moved there for a fresh start after things fell apart in her family. She didn't really have a plan when she got there. All she knew was she needed to get away. Finding a job was not as easy as she had hoped it would be, and she found herself cleaning houses. She didn't enjoy it, but the money was good. With her wages she was able to afford a place in one of the nicer rooming houses in the city. She was proud of herself. She was making it on her own. She felt sane, and most of the people who really knew her were a good distance away. Cassie met Kat about three months after arriving in Jackson while shopping at the Jitney Jungle for one of her employers. Kat made a crude comment about the prunes and Pepto-Bismol in her cart, and Cassie had to explain the items were not hers. The conversation led to Kat offering her a job.

"A sista with no shame can work for me any day," Kat teased. "When you wanna start?" The two became fast friends. Both women cherished their privacy, and each found in the other someone she could trust.

"You do this every year. You the only worker I got who treats my place like a motel. Girl, jus' go see her, or call her on the phone."

Having heard it all before, Cassie got up and brushed past the woman. "Kat, you don't get it. It goes a lot deeper than that."

"Whatever it is, it ain't gon' get solved by gettin' smashed once a year," Kat said, getting the last word.

As Cassie made her way out to the lounge to get her purse from underneath the bar, she went through her activities for the remainder of the day. *I have to be back here at nine tonight. That gives me enough time to stop by and do some chores for Mr. and Mrs. Green.*

"Excuse me, pretty lady," said a velvety voice.

"What can I do for you?" answered Cassie, looking up with surprise that the door was unlocked.

"I'm lookin' for the owner of this here establishment. He around?"

"How you know it's a he?" She grinned flirtatiously at the attractive stranger.

"Forgive me. Is *she* around?" The gentleman flashed a confident smile back at Cassie.

"No, but if you come back tonight round nine o'clock you just might catch her."

"Thank you, pretty lady," he said, turning to leave.

"Sir, you wanna leave your name?" Cassie asked.

"I'll be back at nine," he said with a wink.

"Who were you talkin' to?" asked Kat as she entered the bar.

"Not sure, but he said he'll be back later to see you," she answered, concealing her interest.

"So, where you wanderin' in from?" asked Charlie, giving Ray a sideways glance.

"Here and there. You know I can't let no grass grow underneath these feet. I'ma busy man," answered Ray as he put Baby Lena down. "I gotta keep movin'. I got big plans, Mr. Charlie, and they bigger than this li'l town. Hell, they bigger than the whole state of Mississippi."

"Watch yo' mouth in front these babies," interrupted E. May. She finished cutting the cake and began passing it out. "You stayin' through the night, or do I have to say my goodbyes now?"

"Ma, come on now. Would I just show up and leave like that?"

"Yea!" said everyone in unison.

When Cassie left, Ray started living as a single man. He took jobs that caused him to be absent for random periods of time. No one knew exactly what the work entailed, but his irregular schedule made the family suspicious.

"That's cool, but I plan on bein' around for a li'l while. That's if it's okay with you," he said, looking at Grandpa Charlie. Not waiting for a response, Ray turned his attention to Emma. "Why you so quiet?"

"You don't wanna start with me Ray Walker," she spit back.

"Here, take this cake," said E. May, shoving a plate in Emma's hands.

"Your daddy sure know how to stir up trouble," whispered Helene to Baby Lena as the girls ate their cake.

"Shut up, Helene. You just mad cuz *my* daddy look like a prince and *your* daddy look like the mule he ride on," said Baby Lena, licking icing off her fingers.

"Ooo Lena, why you say that?"

"You talk about my daddy; I talk about yours."

"Hey Mr. Charlie, whatchu know about Mr. Albert selling that plot of land on Route 4?" Ray asked.

Charlie continued to eat his cake and responded without looking up. "Nothin'. And I'ma keep it like that. It ain't right to mix business and friendship. Albert Spears and I been friends since we was boys, and I ain't gon' mess it up by buyin' no land."

"Whatchu mean? I jus' asked a question."

"Yeah, but somehow *you* askin' a question always ends with me spendin' *my* money."

"If I didn't know no betta, I would think y'all don't want me around."

Cough, cough. Emma covered her mouth and cut her eyes at Ray as she stood up to go in the kitchen.

"It's a good thang I ain't neva much cared for what people think." Ray smirked as he watched Emma leave the room.

"Lena and Helene, y'all go put those plates in the sink, and go lay out your clothes for church so you can wash up and go to bed," said E. May, changing the subject.

"But it's my birthday. Can't I stay up longer?" Baby Lena pouted.

"It's gettin' late. And neither one of you is gon' wanna get up in the mornin'. Now go," said E. May, swatting Baby Lena on the behind. "Y'all say good night."

"Good night, Daddy," Lena said. "Good night, everyone else."

"Alright now," said E. May. "My switch don't know it's yo' birthday. Don't be fast-mouthed."

"Yes ma'am," Lena said because she was supposed to and not because she meant it.

As the two girls went off to do as they were told, the adults in the front room gathered around the table. Johnny pulled out the bottle of liquor he had placed in his mama's china cabinet, and Emma returned from the kitchen with cups for everyone except E. May.

"So, what should we drink to?" asked Johnny, the more observant one, who hadn't said anything the entire evening.

"Let's drink to no-good men who get shot in the a-- in the end!" Emma yelled unexpectedly.

"Emma!" said E. May, frustrated by the comment. "Enough!"

"Mama, I'm just—"

"I said, 'enough.'"

"Okay, let's drink to sumthin' a li'l more festive," said Ray, secretly enjoying how upset he could still make Emma. "Let's drink to no-good men who get shot in the a-- in the end and the women who love 'em!"

"You sorry son-of-a—"

"Emma!"

"Mama!"

"Don't fret me! Not one more word, or all you gon' find somewhere else to go," said Charlie, finally fed up.

"That won't be hard for some of us." Emma spoke through clenched teeth. "Some of us are used to sleepin' around."

"Emma!" E. May's voice was louder than usual. "Go check on the girls and make sure they ain't playin' round in that room."

"Why I gotta leave the room? I live here." Emma was ready to finish the fight. "*He's* the guest."

"Emma! Do what yo' mama said!" Charlie stood up from his chair. "Ain't gon' say it again."

Miss Mary Mack!

Mack!

Mack!

All dressed in black!

Black!

Black!

With silver buttons!

"What y'all doin' in here?" said Emma, taking a deep breath as she entered the back bedroom.

"Nothin'," both girls answered.

"What y'all doin' out there?" said Baby Lena without hesitation.

"Lena!" shouted Helene in surprise. The little girl kept her eyes fixed on her aunt in anticipation of a response.

"What? Helene, you heard them fussin' same as me. You know you wanna know what they was talkin' bout too. Auntie Emma, why you hate my daddy so much?" Baby Lena persisted with her interrogation.

Caught completely off guard by the question, Emma tried to focus on the person asking. She loved Baby Lena, and her heart yearned to answer her truthfully. But she knew there was no way she could explain all the details of that relationship. It was much more than Baby Lena needed to know at her age. Still, she laughed as she thought, *But Baby Lena is not your ordinary child.*

"Auntie Emma? Why you hate my daddy so much?"

Forgetting they were waiting for an answer, Emma said matter-of-factly, "Hate and love, it's all the same."

———

Cassie returned to work at Kat's around eight o'clock that night. Ruth Brown's "Mama He Treats Your

Daughter Mean" was playing, and there were a few regulars seated throughout the place. The crowd wouldn't come until after nine o'clock, when they officially opened. Cassie had taken off the sadness of the day before, showered, and freshened her face. She decided to wear her baby-blue hot pants with a white blouse and white leather vest. Her shape was accentuated in that outfit, and she could use the extra tips. She walked to the back to put her bag on the sofa where she had slept the night before.

"Check you out, all dressed up," said Kat. "You must be expectin' someone special to come through them doors."

"Girl, whatchu talkin' bout? It's Saturday night, and I'm tryna' shake off yesterday," she said. She wouldn't dare tell Kat about wanting extra tips. Kat was her friend, but Cassie knew business always came first for Kat. The only thing more important than making money to Kat was not losing it to someone else.

"Ohhh, okay. I thought you might be preparin' for yo' mystery man," Kat replied.

"Chile, please. That man was here on business; probably tryna' sell sumthin'. He may not even come back." She avoided eye contact as she said this. The truth was Cassie had not stopped thinking about him since their first meeting. She wondered who he was and what he was doing in Mississippi.

Cassie returned to the front of the lounge, grabbed an apron from behind the counter, got her tray ready, and began checking the supply of glasses. She was interrupted about an hour later.

"Hey, pretty lady. Glad to see you again," said the familiar voice from earlier.

Cassie looked up and saw the stranger watching her with a sly smile on his face. Captivated by his smooth chocolate skin, she followed his lips as they formed the words, "It's nine o'clock."

She blushed and fumbled over her words. "I sssee, and you on time."

He chuckled, sensing her nervousness. "Is the owner here?"

Trying to gain her composure, Cassie leaned in flirtatiously and replied, "Depends. Who shall I say is here?"

"Just tell him a man from Chicago wants to talk business. There's an opportunity I think he'll be interested in."

"Wait here while I go get *her*," she said.

Realizing he was watching her walk away, she turned back and said, "Don't go nowhere." As she made her way into the back, Cassie called out, "Kat!

The mystery man is back! He out front, and he wanna talk to you. Says it's about business and you could make a lot of money. He says he's from Chicago." Cassie found Kat in the kitchen at the table, measuring out the liquor for the night. She kept the bottles half full because she believed people drank more when they thought the supply was running low.

Looking up over her glasses, Kat said, "Oh really? And just what does this mystery man from Chicago want in exchange for makin' *me* a lot of money?"

Anxious to get back to him, Cassie said, "I don't know, but he wants to talk to you. You comin'?"

"Tell him I'll be there in a minute." Having been raised by her father in a home connected to a bar made Kat streetwise. She was a tall, nice-looking woman with youthful-looking brown skin. She had a beautiful smile that she rarely shared with others and shiny, hazel eyes. She grew up hearing men and women cuss and fight after too many drinks. And she watched her father play counselor and best friend to the forgotten in their community. When he died, she felt obligated to keep the place open. Kat learned early on how she would have to behave to be taken seriously. She didn't get friendly with customers, and when she went to buy liquor or someone came trying to sell her some, she kept the conversations short. No laughter and no small talk. She always wore pants and a black newsboy cap that had belonged to her dad. While she was lonely for companionship, she enjoyed the freedom of being her own boss, and secretly she enjoyed the idea of men desiring her and believing they couldn't have her.

Kat had a small family and spent a lot of time alone. She wasn't looking to befriend Cassie when she hired her, but Cassie ignored the wall she had put up to keep people out. Cassie was like the sister she never had, but Kat would never tell her that. Yet, she felt Cassie already knew.

Cassie returned to the bar and found the mystery man seated, peeling a boiled egg. "Can I get you sumthin' to drink with that?"

"Whatchu got?" he asked, looking up. He hadn't realized how beautiful she was. Her eyes were stunning yet sad.

"I'll give you the house special," Cassie said, pulling the bottle from underneath the counter and pouring him a glass.

"What's in it?" He nodded his approval and took another sip.

"Can't tell. It's a secret," she replied, putting her finger to her lips. "It's the best drink in Jackson, though. Kat said give her a minute, and she'll be out."

"Kat? You weren't jivin'," he said amazed and fascinated. "The owner really is a woman."

"You still ain't told me your name," Cassie asked again.

"Later," he said, turning his attention to the woman who had joined them.

"I'm Kat. I understand you wanna talk to me," she said, taking control of the conversation. "Follow me to my office." Kat coolly led him to a small wobbly table in the corner of the room. "So, what's this about?"

"Well, I can see you like to get down to it," he said, studying her every move. "Me and my partners got some business here in Jackson once or twice a month, and we lookin' for someone who wouldn't mind playin' host to us. A place we could call a home away from home and not have to look over our shoulders. Catch my drift?"

"In case you haven't noticed, this is a bar for average workin' folks. We don't get a lot of high rollers, hustlers and such in here, and not sure I want any." Kat folded her arms and sat back in her chair.

"Look, we don't wanna bring no bad element in here. We jus' need a place to meet that's low key, and we'll pay you for your time." Ace was unsure which approach to take. This woman didn't seem to notice his charm, but he didn't want to offend her by treating her like a man.

"So, you expect me to believe you and yo' partners will come through here once or twice a month and 'meet,' and no bad element will follow? Mr. Chicago, I don't know what kind of 'business' you in or how much money you offerin', but I'm gon' have to pass.

"Miss Kat, you a smart woman, so I'm gon' say it like this. We run a few small gamblin' houses for those in these parts who want a taste of the city life. But right now, we workin' on sumthin' big that could make the right people a lot of money. Really, Miss. Kat, we just a few brothas tryna' stay one step ahead of the man."

Softening because of his honesty, Kat responded, "Let me think about it. How much we talkin'?"

"Name your price," he smiled confidently.

"Come back tomorrow, and I'll let you know."

"On Sunday?" He was confused by this.

"Come for your answer tomorrow around two o'clock." Kat stood up and walked away.

Left sitting alone, he wondered about this woman and the whole encounter. He was impressed with the way she handled herself, and this made him think she could be more useful than previously planned. His thoughts were interrupted by a sweet voice.

"You wanna another drink?" Cassie stood over his shoulder with a glass in her hand. "How'd it go?" she asked, taking a seat. "You ready to tell me your name?"

"Not just yet." He finished his drink as he stood up. "Let's see what happens tomorrow."

"Tomorrow?" She was puzzled.

"Tomorrow," he said as he walked out the door.

Cassie watched the mystery man leave as smoothly as he had come in. While she sat with her opposing feelings, she could hear Marvin Gaye's "Pride and Joy" from the jukebox.

Any danger she suspected was minimized by her curiosity and fascination. As Cassie collected herself and headed back to the bar to tend to her customers, she whispered to herself, "Tomorrow."

"Well?" asked the driver of the car.

"She's a tough broad, but I think she'll do business," said the mystery man, getting into a silver Thunderbird that was waiting outside. "We comin' back tomorrow for her answer."

"She? Tomorrow? Ace, man, you gettin' soft. First you let that small-time country hood rip us off, and now you got some chick callin' the shots on how we do business! Man, I don't get it."

"Look, Eddie, leave this to me. I know women, and that Miss Kat is a smart one. She could be very good for business."

"Well, what'd he say?" Cassie asked Kat later that evening as they were straightening up the tables and chairs.

"Said he wanted to use my place as a meeting spot for business."

"Meetings. What'd you say?"

"Told him I'd think on it and give him an answer tomorrow."

"Ohhh, that's what he meant. He's comin back here tomorrow for your answer. Whatchu gon' tell him?"

"I dunno."

CHAPTER TWO

That breakfast sho' smell good. I could eat me about five pieces of bacon," said Charlie as he entered the kitchen rubbing his stomach and kissing E. May on the cheek. "You still know how to wake a man in the mornin'. Where everybody at? They can't smell all this good food?"

"The girls washin' up. Can't say where Freddy went to this mornin'. Johnny went around to Aunt Ethel's and Uncle Otto's. Emma still sleep; thank the Lawd. And Ray is where Ray usually is—gone."

"Gone? Before breakfast? Humph, that's strange, even for him."

"Mornin', Grandmama! Mornin', Granddaddy!" the girls sang.

"Grandma, where my daddy?" asked Baby Lena as she and Helene climbed into the chairs at the table. "He done ate already?"

"Naw baby. Yo' daddy not here," said E. May, trying to hide her own disappointment.

"Told you he wouldn't be here when you woke up," said Helene, eating her bacon.

"Shut up, Helene, or you won't be here when I wake up!" Baby Lena snapped.

"That don't even make sense!" Helene laughed.

"Your face don't make sense," Baby Lena replied, laughing too.

For as long as Baby Lena could remember, she and Helene had gone back and forth. Helene was her favorite cousin and best friend, and although Helene was nine years old, Baby Lena still told her what to do. Helene was Johnny's daughter. When Helene's mother died in childbirth, Johnny moved back to Pinola to be with his parents. He needed help raising Helene and getting through his grief. Johnny moved in with his brother, Freddy, in the double-wide trailer that sat behind their parent's house, and Helene moved into the house with E. May, Charlie, Emma, Cassie, Ray and Baby Lena.

Helene was a shy and awkward child with sandy-brown features. It was as if her hair and skin were the same color. The two fussed all the time, but they couldn't stand to be apart from each other. Baby Lena was vocal and rambunctious; Helene was cautious and reserved. However, she was more outgoing when she was with Baby Lena.

"Ya'll stop all that and eat yo' breakfast so we can get ready for church," said E. May. "Don't make me late. I gotta sing this mornin', and I don't wanna have to come out that choir stand because the two of you actin' up.

"I won't," said Helene still enjoying her breakfast. "Lena might though."

"You jus' mind yo'self li'l girl, and let Baby Lena mind hers," said E. May, noticing Baby Lena's silence. "You get enough to eat, chile?"

"Yes ma'am," she responded, not really listening. She was wondering where her daddy had gone. *Was he alright? Did they have another fight last night after she and Helene had gone to sleep? Was he coming back?*

"But you ain't touched them grits and eggs, and I know they yo' favorite."

"I just ain't hungry right now," Baby Lena said, shuffling the food around the plate with her fork.

"Baby, wherever yo' daddy is, he alright. He know how to take care of himself," E. May said softly.

"Oh hell! What time is it?" said Ray blinded by the sunlight streaming through the window. "Get up! It's mornin'! Emma, get up!"

"What, Ray?" said an annoyed Emma, rubbing the sleep out of her eyes. "You in my bed, remember? You gon' have to find yo' way back to where you was sleepin' and hope you don't get caught."

"Where my pants?" he said, ignoring her and searching the floor as quietly as he could.

"They over here on my side where you left 'em," she said, twirling them around and then tossing them in his direction. "Ray, calm down. Just put your pants on and ease back out. You know they probably in the kitchen eatin' breakfast." Emma enjoyed watching Ray nervously scramble around. As much as he angered her, she still loved him. No matter how much time passed, whenever they came together, they always found their way into each other's arms. It was as if their bodies were meant for each other. Emma felt deep down that Ray was the reason she had never married. She secretly belonged to him and always would.

Ray slipped his pants and shirt on and peeked out the door. Hearing voices down the hall, he left Emma's room and tiptoed back to his room next door. Luckily, everyone was in the kitchen. Feeling confident no one had seen him, Ray changed his shirt, slapped on some cologne, brushed his hair back, put on his shoes, and climbed out the window. He figured he would stay gone for a while and return later in the day.

———◆———

"Praise the Lord!"

"Hallelujah!"

"Thank you Jesus!"

"Amen!"

The church was as warm in spirit as the actual temperature inside. With no air conditioner the large fans fought a losing battle against the steamy wind that blew through the open windows. The church wasn't large like some country churches, but First Peace Baptist was always crowded. Baby Lena and Helene sat on the same pew every Sunday, directly facing their grandmother in the choir stand so she could keep an eye on them. This particular morning each girl had her hair combed in two ponytails, one on each side. They wore light yellow dresses with white ankle socks and black patent leather shoes. Their Aunt Emma loved to dress them alike, and the girls didn't mind.

"You want a peppermint?" Baby Lena whispered to Helene.

"Where you get peppermint from?" she whispered back.

"Do you wanna a piece or not?" Baby Lena said.

"Yeah, but I still wanna know where you got it from," Helene said, trying to keep her eyes looking forward.

"I ain't tellin'. Here, take it," said Baby Lena, pulling the mint out of her pocket.

"You got one for you?" asked Helene.

"Yeah, I got two more. Now shut up before Grandma come down here."

There was as much activity outside the church and as there was inside. Every Sunday those who didn't make it all the way in would park their cars in the school parking lot next door. It was an unofficial meeting spot for all the black sheep of every local family to gather and be near their families who had gone inside. Outside they stood around and talked about old times, many of them reminiscing about their glory days on the basketball or baseball team. They told stories and often had to tell each other to quiet down when they got too loud. They never cursed, and they never smoked or drank during these weekly gatherings. The women stood around listening. Some engaged in their own light conversations about current gossip. Women who were single hoped to get noticed, while those in relationships made sure to stake their claims.

None of the Smith children dared to be found outside with this group. No matter how bad their lives got, they knew better than to disrespect their family name and their faith.

Ray turned the corner and headed down the hill. In the distance he could see the group at the school and hear the sounds from inside and outside the church. As he walked, he thought about Emma. Deep down, he felt guilty that maybe his trip to see his baby girl wasn't really about Baby Lena after all. He and Emma had a history they couldn't shake. No matter what happened in life, they always found their way back to each other. But for Ray, Baby Lena's birth had made everything more complicated. He felt like every time he tried to get on the straight and narrow, something came along to knock him off course. Yes, he loved women, but he was ready to settle down and raise his family. He just didn't know who with.

"Well, well, well. Look what the wind blew in," said a young man as Ray approached. "Give me some skin."

"What's happenin', Will Lee? Been a long time," Ray said.

Will Lee and Ray had grown up together. As kids they were thick as thieves. As they got older, Will Lee tried to make an honest living, but he enjoyed the money and excitement of stealing. He was a nice-looking man, with an innocent face that made his victims easy prey. He was quick and calculating, so no one ever knew what he was plotting behind his smile. Ray also enjoyed the excitement of the fast life, but he had standards. He only cheated or stole from people he regarded as criminals already. "I take what's been taken," he often said.

"Man, you tell me. The word is you got yo'self into some trouble up there in Jackson and that's why you came back down here." Will Lee stood up from the car trunk he'd been sitting on. "They say you hit those snake eyes one too many times and didn't pay up. Any truth to that?"

"Listen, them fools cheated me! I ain't payin' up on no loaded dice," Ray said.

"Well, you betta hope they don't come knockin' on Mr. Charlie's door. I heard they some big-time playas here from Chicago, and they damn sure ain't gon' let no country boy cheat 'em out they bread. By the way, how's Emma?" said Will Lee with a wide grin.

"It was Baby Lena's birthday yesterday. That's why I'm here. Look, what you know about Mr. Albert selling that plot of land over there off Route 4?"

"Nothin' much. Far as I figure, he gettin' old and ain't got much use for it since his wife died. None of his kids come down here much anymore either."

"How much he askin'?"

"Why, ni--a? You ain't got no money! Look, if I hear anything I'll let you know. That's if you still around," Will Lee said, eyeing his old friend.

"I'll be around." Ray said this confidently, but he didn't really believe himself.

"Man, where you headed?" Will Lee asked, changing his tone.

"Nowhere in particular. Why?"

"Cuz church about to let out, and I know you don't want Miss E. May and Mr. Charlie to see you out here. You ain't no Smith by blood, but you might as well be."

"Yeah, I hear you," he said, looking toward the church door. "Listen, I'll check you later. Maybe I'll get over to the house sometime tomorrow."

"Brotha, you take it easy out here," said Will Lee, giving his friend a strong handshake.

As church ended E. May collected the girls and headed for the exit where Pastor Jones was standing greeting congregants as they left. The girls always joked to themselves, "Y'all hurry along now. I need to get supper on," mimicking their grandmother. E. May would say this many times before she actually made it outside. As they reached the door of the church, the girls stepped outside and waited as Grandma E. May talked to the pastor. Grandpa Charlie always seemed to make it to the car first. Baby Lena smiled to herself as she saw her daddy's silhouette walking off in the distance. *I knew he wasn't gone*, she thought.

———◆———

"How was church?" asked Emma as they came into the kitchen.

"It was good. We missed you though," said E. May. "But at least you got supper started. Y'all go take off them church clothes."

"Grandma, can we go outside and play?" asked Baby Lena.

"Yeah, but y'all stay round this house."

"Okay," they said in agreement.

"Let me get out of these clothes, and I'll help you finish gettin' the food on," E. May said to Emma. As if liberating herself, E. May stepped out of her shoes and took off her hat there in the kitchen.

Emma continued mixing the potato salad. She hoped her mother didn't ask her a lot of questions. She didn't feel like being lectured, and she certainly didn't feel like being embarrassed. For the first time, she really felt ashamed for being with Ray. She didn't know why. Maybe it was Baby Lena's question the night before. She was sure no one knew what they had done, but somehow her mother's words always managed to convict her. *How long would the family carry all these secrets to keep up appearances?* Emma felt ready to burst. *Maybe it was time that everything came out in the open.*

"Auntie, can we have a popsicle?" asked Baby Lena, disrupting Emma's thoughts.

"Just one?" Emma cracked back.

"Nooo, one for her and one for me," Baby Lena giggled.

"Here, y'all take 'em outside. I don't want no sticky popsicle juice on the floor."

"Thank you, Auntie," they said leaving Emma to her thoughts.

"I prayed for yo' sister today," said E. May, coming into the kitchen. "She been on my mind real heavy. I hope she alright."

"Mama, Cassie can take care of herself," said Emma. "Besides, no one told her to go."

"I ain't so sure. Seems to me we got a whole lotta blame to spread around for what happened to her and this family, and you and Ray get the biggest share.

But that ain't what got me worried. I keep havin' these dreams. I see her, and she always got some kind of dark shadow followin' her. Like sumthin' wrong. You and yo' brothers need to go and check on her."

"Mama, she won't wanna see us," Emma insisted.

"Just go by that house to see if she still there."

"Okay, I'll ask Johnny when he get home."

———

"Good afternoon, Miss Kat," said Ace as he opened the door to the bar. He could see her sitting at the same table from the night before. He felt she looked different in the daylight. Her features and body language seemed more delicate and welcoming.

"You on time," she said lighting a cigarette. "I like that."

"A good businessman always is," he smiled, turning on the charm as he slid into the chair.

"Can I get you a drink?" She shocked herself as she asked him. She never got too friendly when conducting business.

"Naw, but thanks. Even a sinner tries to take one day off," he winked. "So, Miss Kat, my partners and I are anxious to know your decision. You interested in doin' business?"

"Mr. Chicago, I'll play ball. Just for a li'l' while. I can use the extra bread. But let's be clear: The first sign of trouble, and I'm callin' the whole thing off. The deal is you pay me $300 a month, and turn me on to yo' liquor connections, so I can get the good stuff cheap."

"That can be arranged," he nodded. "Miss Kat, I'm sure as time go on, you'll see that this deal will be good for all of us. My name is Ace by the way," he said, extending a hand.

"Nice to meet you, Ace," she said, taking his hand and smiling for the first time.

"I'll bring my boys by one day soon so you can meet 'em. We'll stop in once a month or so to conduct some business, leave you your money, and be on our way. Treat us like any other customers. If you wanna talk jus' hand me a note, and we can set sumthin' up."

"It's gon' be real hard for y'all to blend in around here. Folks know their neighbors," she said, sounding skeptical. "But I'll go along with it…for now."

"Miss Kat, trust me. This'll be the easiest money you eva made."

"Mr. Chicago, I mean Ace, easy money ain't neva easy."

The two said their goodbyes, Ace leaving out the front door and Kat remaining at the table finishing her cigarette. She knew there was much more to Ace and his partners. They were probably into prostitution and drugs, but she also knew she couldn't afford to keep her place open with the money it was making.

As Ace got in the Thunderbird waiting around the corner, he was met with, "How'd it go?"

"I told you to trust me. Everything is solid," Ace replied.

"So, she went along with the whole arrangement? Even the drop off of the dope?"

"Eddie, man, I told you. It's all taken care of."

"Alright Mr. Smooth, but you still ain't told me what we gon' do about that country boy who owe us money. We don't want these folks thinkin' we can't take care of business."

"Hold up a minute," said Ace, getting out of the car. "Good afternoon, Miss Lady," he said, walking toward Cassie.

"Good afternoon ya'self," she said pleasantly surprised.

"You work on Sundays?"

"Not usually, but I needed to stop by and see Kat."

"You sure that's the only reason you comin' around this time of day?" He flashed a slick grin.

"I'm sorry; I don't follow," she said, playing coy.

Honk, honk, honk! Honk honk!

"Man, come on! We got places to be!" yelled Eddie from the car.

"The name is Ace," he said, tipping a pretend hat.

"Well, nice to meet you Ace. I'm Cassie," she blushed.

"I'll be seein' you," he said, running back to the car.

Cassie watched as Ace got in the car and it made a U-turn, going back up the road.

"Ace," she said to herself. "I like that."

As the Thunderbird made its way toward Terry Road, it passed a brown Buick Skylark. Inside Emma, Johnny, and Freddy were arguing about which turn to take next.

"I told you not to come this way," said a frustrated Emma.

"Look, if you know so much, you could've drove yo'self," said Johnny. "It didn't take all three of us to come up here."

"She all our sister," Emma snapped. "And besides, that's what Mama wanted. Now take it up with her."

"Look! There she go, right there!" said Freddy.

Johnny honked the horn and pulled over to the side of the road. Still in a daze, Cassie didn't immediately recognize the three people in the car.

"What they want?" she said annoyed.

As she started in the opposite direction, Freddy jumped out and ran to her. "Look, I know you don't wanna see us, but Mama worried about you. And you know how she get when she get sumthin' on her mind. She feel like you in some kind of trouble."

"Trouble? What kind of trouble? The only trouble I've ever had came from the people who were supposed to love me. Look, I appreciate y'all takin' the drive, but you can leave now. I'm fine."

"Do you need anything?" asked Freddy, feeling sad for how his family had treated Cassie.

"No, y'all have done enough. How's Baby Lena? Did she have a good birthday?" Cassie changed the subject.

"Yeah, but I know she miss you," he said, not sure if he should tell her Ray was back.

"Freddy, tell her I love her." Her voice cracked as she held back her tears. "I gotta go. Tell Mama I'm doin' fine."

"Cassie, please come home and tell her ya'self." Freddie could see the sadness in his sister's eyes.

"I can't. Not until we ready to lay it all out and face the truth. I been hurt, and Baby Lena been hurt more," she said as she backed up and walked away. "Not until we ready to talk about the lies been told and the secret we been hidin' for seven years."

"Love you Cass," said Freddy, calling after her.

"I love you too," she said, not turning around.

"What did she say?" asked Emma as Freddy got in the car.

"She said to tell Baby Lena, she loves her, and tell Mama she's okay."

"That's all? That's it?" she asked.

"Emma, for the rest of the ride back don't say nothin'. Alright? Just sit there and ride," Freddy said.

Emma sank back in her seat and folded her arms. She was quiet for the rest of the trip.

CHAPTER THREE

"Boss, it's cool. These country folk starvin' for some real action, and we got us a nice little setup," said Ace, looking at his watch. "Look, man, don't listen to Eddie. We got it all under control. This Ace you talkin' to. You know I'ma take care of it. Alright…later."

Ace hung up the phone. His mind went immediately to seeing Cassie earlier. She was the most beautiful woman he had ever met. She was vulnerable but strong, innocent but worldly, naïve but alert. Her complexity captivated him, and he wanted to get to know her better.

Ace was a handsome man with a tall frame. His eyes were bright with thick lashes. His voice was deep and silky. Born in Alabama but raised in Chicago, he learned the street life early on, watching his father go in and out of jail for petty crimes and con jobs gone wrong. So, he grew up determined to beat the system and be a better criminal than his father was. He began hanging around the neighborhood thugs as a youngster, and as he got older he hung around the numbers runners and spent time in the nightclubs. As a child, the kids teased him all the time, saying he was "as black as the ace of spades." As a teen he embraced it and nicknamed himself "Ace." It took hold, so much so, that few people outside his family knew his real name.

When he was about seventeen, he met and began to work for Double T, who became the father figure he longed for. Ace was both likeable and arrogant because he was good-looking and able to talk his way out of most situations. He regularly made it known that while he had been stopped by police many times and even arrested on several occasions, he never spent more than a night in jail. Ace had never been married, and he had no children that he was aware of or claimed. He was a private person, never talking about his mother, father, or two sisters. He learned from Double T that in their line of work, it's not a good idea to get too personal or too attached.

"Cassie," he said to himself. "I like that."

"Boy, you been gone all day. Missed supper and all. Where you been?" said Charlie to Ray as he walked onto the porch.

"I was out visitin' some old friends," said Ray, taking a seat next to the old man. "Where everybody at?"

"E. May and the girls in the house, and Emma and the boys went to Jackson to check on *yo'* wife." He said the last part looking directly at Ray.

"Jackson? Did sumthin' happen?"

"Naw. E. May made 'em go. Sumthin' bout a bad dream."

"A bad dream?"

"Yeah, E. May dreamt sumthin' happened to Cassie, and she sent them to check on her."

"Where she stayin?"

"Can't say. Last I heard she was workin' for some teacher and his wife."

Ray felt a churning in his stomach that he couldn't explain. "Mr. Charlie, excuse me," he said, getting up to go inside.

"Mama E. May, what's this I hear about you havin' bad dreams about Cassie?" asked Ray as he saw the woman sitting in the front room.

"Just a feelin' is all. You know how us old folks get. Seem like the good Lawd tryna' prepare you for sumthin'." E. May was staring into space rocking back and forth. "Ray, it's time we put things back in order. If me and Charlie had paid more attention to our family than to what people would say, things would be different. Cassie would be home, and Baby Lena would know who her real mama is.

"Ray, take it from me, secrets and lies don't do nothin' but eat you up from the inside out. I done asked God to forgive me, and I believe He has, but we gotta make this right. Too many people been hurt behind all this mess."

"Yes ma'am, but ain't Baby Lena too young for all this? Shouldn't we wait for her to get a li'l older?" he said, feeling sicker.

"Chile, ain't no *good* age to have your heart broke. No matter when you tell her, it's gon' hurt."

———◆———

"I de-clare war!" said the girls, playing cards on the bed.

"It's my turn to deal," said Helene.

"Okay, but can you keep a secret?" asked Baby Lena still shuffling the cards

"Lena, I keep all yo' secrets," said Helene. She gently grabbed the cards from Baby Lena.

"Yeah, but this a big secret. Sooo big you could get the switch just knowin' about it," Baby Lena whispered.

"What, Lena?" asked Helene.

"Promise you won't tell? Cross your heart and hope to die, stick a needle in your eye?"

"I cross my heart and hope to die, stick a needle in my eye," said Helene, crossing two fingers over her heart.

"You remember those mints we ate in church?"

"Yeahh."

"I snuck and took 'em from off Auntie Emma's dresser this mornin'."

"So? Why's that a secret?"

"That ain't the secret, dummy!" She leaned in closer to Helene. "The secret is there was somebody else in the room besides Auntie Emma."

"Oooh, Lena! You fast-mouthed!" said Helene, getting loud.

"Shut up, Helene! I ain't do nothin'. I'm just tellin' what I saw," said Baby Lena, putting her hand over the girl's mouth.

"Lena! I'ma tell Grandma E. May!"

"Helene, hush. You know how mad she can get. She'll be mad at you, me, *and* Auntie Emma. See, that's why I'm not gon' tell you nothin' else." She said this knowing it would keep Helene from talking.

"Who was it, Lena?" said Helene, calming down.

"I don't know. All I saw was two big bumps in the bed," she said. "Remember, you promised. Don't say nothin' to nobody."

"Auntie Emma gon' get you, she know you been in her room and seen her," said Helene.

"I ain't gon' tell her, and *you* ain't gon' tell her, so how she gon' know?"

"She gon' know cuz her mints is gone," said Helene confidently.

"I still ain't gon' say nothin'. I ain't the only one who takes mints from her dresser. Uncle Johnny, Uncle Freddy, and Grandpa, all of 'em go in there. She ain't gon' know it's me." Baby Lena hoped to herself she was right.

The girls could hear voices and the screen door being opened and closed in the front. Emma, Johnny, and Freddy had returned from Jackson, and everyone gathered in the front room to hear the news.

"Did you see her?" asked E. May. "Was she alright? What'd she say?"

"Mama, we saw her," said Freddy. "She said she alright. Told us to tell you she love you and not to worry."

"That's all?" E. May was perplexed. "Where she livin'? Does she make enough money to support herself? When she comin' home?"

"Mama," said Freddy, "we didn't talk that long. She didn't wanna see us. She said she doin' fine, and that's it. Sorry."

"Lawd, my chile. She need to come home," her voice more desperate. "Charlie, our baby needs to come home."

"Calm down, May. We'll work it out," said Charlie, not sure what else to say. "Me and you'll take a ride up there, okay? Then you can see for yo'self."

PART II

CHAPTER FOUR

Three months had gone by since Ace and his boys began their monthly meetings at Kat's Place. And just as he promised, there was no interruption in her business. To the contrary, business was picking up. And it was a younger, hipper clientele than the neighborhood regulars. Kat felt the new business required her to make some much needed upgrades, so she bought a new sign and some matching chairs for the tables. She updated the music in the jukebox and rearranged the room to provide more space for dancing. She even added one of those fancy lights that changed colors. The arrangement was for $300 a month, but Ace made sure to always add an extra $100 here and there. Kat's Place was becoming a popular spot on Raymond Road. What she didn't know was her speculations were true. Her place was being used in an elaborate system to supply dope to Ace's more sophisticated clients.

Ace had four young men from the area, all between the ages of seventeen and twenty-five, to run his drugs. They were groomed with aspirations and promises of running the city, having the finest women, and driving the best cars. These young men worked different areas around town, and they were given specific instructions not to make Miss Kat aware of their dealings. They entertained themselves and their friends at Kat's, so they could easily be found by Ace whenever needed. During their monthly meetings Ace, along with Eddie and their other colleagues, would meet mostly to collect money.

"What y'all drinking this evening?" Cassie asked, looking directly at Ace. "Is it the house special all around?"

"Yeah baby, that'll be cool," he said winking at her.

As Cassie left the table, all the men watched her walk away. "Mmm. Mmm. Mmm. She is out of sight! Ace, man, you betta make yo' move before anotha brotha slide in and take that," Eddie said slyly. "I'm surprised you takin' this long."

"Man, talk about sh-t you know. That's already mine," Ace responded, keeping his eyes on Cassie.

"That's cool, brotha," said Eddie, getting up. "I'ma step outside to grab this bread. Some of us still remember there's work to do."

As Eddie got up, Cassie returned with the drinks. "Here you go. One for you, one for you, and one for him." She made sure to brush against Ace as she placed his glass on the table.

"What time you get off tonight?" Ace asked Cassie. "I wanna take you someplace nice."

She had always found an excuse each time Ace had asked her to go out. "It'll be awful late, and by the time I help clean up it will be well after 1:00 a.m. And besides, there's only a few places open that time of mornin' and ain't none of 'em nice."

"Miss Cassie don't go gettin' offended," he said, putting his hand on hers. "I jus' wanna take you for a drive. Maybe we go to the park, sit and watch the sun come up. You keep turnin' me down you gon' make me think you don't like me." He moved in closer and gave her a smile. "And we both know that ain't true."

"Maybe some other time," she said coolly, fighting the urge to say 'yes'. Her attraction to Ace was so strong it scared her. She hadn't felt like that for anyone except Ray, and the consequences of that relationship were still haunting her. And even though she worked at Kat's, Cassie couldn't abandon or ignore her upbringing. Ace's lifestyle appeared to be everything she was taught to avoid.

"Okay, I'll let you turn me down this last time. The next time will be a 'yes.'" He said this confidently, but deep down he was disappointed and concerned she might not really like him.

———————

After tossing and turning for an hour, E. May quietly got out of bed so as not to disturb Charlie. She considered making herself some hot tea but decided to go outside instead. As the breeze gently brushed her skin, she began to relax. Hearing only the sounds of nature and her own breathing she rested in the rocking chair. Not saying a word at first, the tears began to roll down her face as she began to pray.

"Gracious Lawd, I come to you as humbly as I know how on behalf of my family. Lawd, my heart is heavy and my mind is troubled. We need you Father. There's been a lot of lies told, and now my family is hurtin'. We can't move forward or move on cuz we ain't free. Lawd, I ask for yo' forgiveness for all the lies been said. Lies been said to you, ourselves and each other. Lawd, we was wrong for carin' more about what people think then the truth. And we was wrong for keepin' a secret from Baby Lena. Now there's a chile that don't know who her real mama is, and my Cassie out in the world thinkin' her family don't love her. Lawd, keep her safe, and let her not be guided by her own broken heart. Keep us all safe Father. And forgive us our trespasses as we forgive the ones who trespass against us. Help us not to be afraid to tell the truth, so we can be free of the hurt and pain it's done caused us. Restore our family with the love and togetherness we used to have. Thank you, merciful Father. In the sweet name of Jesus I pray, amen."

E. May finished her prayer and sat for a long while, rocking and breathing, breathing and rocking. She knew she would be able to rest now.

As closing time came, Cassie collected the dirty glasses and placed them on the back counter for them to be washed for the next night. She collected the empty bottles and took them into the kitchen in the back so Kat could refill them. She wondered how much longer Kat would keep doing that, given how much money she was making now.

Cassie wiped down the bar, put the chairs back in place, and swept the floor. As she was finishing, she decided to put some money in the jukebox. She rarely thought to play the music she wanted to hear, so she selected "Misty Blue," a song by Dorothy Moore, a singer from right there in Jackson.

Cassie sang along, using the broom as a microphone. As she swayed back and forth, entertaining her imaginary audience, a voice interrupted her. "May I join you?"

Turning toward the door, Cassie saw Ace standing there. Before she could ask him how he got in there, he took the broom from her and gently pulled her in for a dance. With his arms locked around her waist, Cassie settled in, resting her arms on his and her head on his chest. Ace sang softly in her ear as they moved to the music.

Still dancing after the song stopped, Ace continued to hum the melody. Their dance ended when Ace loosened his hold around her waist, looked down into her eyes, and kissed her. It was the most passionate yet sensitive kiss she had ever experienced. She felt weightless in that moment. Like her body had been set free from the pain of her broken heart. As if everything that had her weighed down had been released.

"Thank you for the dance, Miss Cassie," he said in her ear as he hugged her close to say good night.

"Thank you," she said, kissing his cheek.

As they stepped away from each other, Ace once again left as smoothly as he had entered. Cassie locked the door and returned to her sweeping.

CHAPTER FIVE

It was Saturday morning, and E. May was up cleaning the house. The girls had spent the night at their Uncle Otto and Aunt Ethel's house. They were there to play with their cousins who had come from out of town. Emma was still in bed, and Charlie, Johnny, and Freddy were outside working on one of Charlie's cars. E. May felt refreshed from the night before, and she hummed to herself as she changed the sheets on the bed.

As she fluffed the pillow, her mind went back to the day Emma told her she was pregnant with Ray's baby. E. May had had a feeling the two of them had been fooling around, but she didn't want to believe it. She certainly never imagined it would result in Emma getting pregnant. Hearing that, she remembered going into survival mode. How to protect herself and her family from the scandal and shame that would come. Ray being unfaithful to Cassie and Emma becoming pregnant by her sister's husband was all too much to grasp. So, she and Charlie got Emma, Ray and Cassie together, and they instructed them that the sisters would be going to Memphis to stay with their Aunt Peggie until the baby was born. E. May never asked Cassie how she felt, and she never gave Emma and Ray the scolding they deserved. The sisters rode to Memphis on the train and stayed there fifteen months. Emma gave birth to Charlena Raynee Walker on July 13, 1970. When Baby Lena was six months old, Ray, Johnny and Freddy drove to Memphis to bring them all home. Upon returning to Pinola, Cassie raised Baby Lena as her child with Ray. This would be the family's secret.

Things seemed to be going fine until Emma became jealous of Cassie. She made sure to criticize Cassie's parenting at every turn. Emma felt her big sister had it all: her baby and her man. Sometime before Baby Lena's third birthday, Emma and Ray resumed their affair. It was confirmed the day Cassie smelled her sister's perfume on one of Ray's shirts. This sent Cassie over the edge. She already felt guilty for raising Baby Lena as her own, but she was furious that no one in her family seemed to notice or speak out against Emma and Ray's continued infidelity. So, Cassie, feeling like she was having a nervous break-down, wrapped up Baby Lena, gathered up some of their clothes, and walked up the road to Will Lee's place. After some convincing, he drove her to the bus station in Mendenhall. As Ray's best friend, Will Lee already knew what was going on. And because he always liked Cassie, he felt obligated to help her. Leaving with Baby Lena scared the whole household. And Ray and Emma, who were both angry, began to blame each other. That morning, when Ray revealed to Will Lee that Cassie was gone with his child, Will Lee confessed to helping her leave by taking her to the station.

Ray was furious at Cassie as he drove to retrieve her and his baby girl. Once at the bus station, he got out and cursed Cassie, telling her he would call the police and have her locked up for being crazy. Feeling defeated, Cassie got in the car with Ray and returned home with him. The next time Cassie left; she went alone.

"Ma!!! Where you at?" called Emma.

"I'm in here changin' the sheets!" she said, coming out of her daze.

"I been callin' you. You ain't hear me?" asked Emma, standing at the door.

"Must not have if I ain't answer."

"Whatchu doin?"

"Can't you see I'm makin' the bed?" E. May was still distracted by her thoughts. "I jus' got to thinkin' bout yo' sister, Baby Lena, *you*, and Ray. It's time to fix the mess we made."

"Mama, please—," Emma started to say.

"Don't 'Mama' me. It's time to mend fences. We all gotta admit our wrong and ask for forgiveness. It's time to get it right. Baby Lena growin' up, and she need to know where she come from."

"Do we have to do this today? Right now?" Emma asked.

"Emma, it ain't goin' away. No matta how you try and act like it ain't happen, it did happen. And now you payin'. Cassie payin'. We all payin'. And worst off, Baby Lena payin'. I can't tell you when and where, but you betta do it befo' it's too late."

"Mama, there you go," said Emma fearfully. "What's about to happen? You not tryna' leave here, are you?" She sat down in a chair near her mother.

"We all gotta go, but that's not what I'm talkin' 'bout. You can't take people for granted cuz you neva know when you gon' get a chance to say 'I'm sorry.' And you got lots to be sorry for." E. May looked piercingly into Emma's eyes. "What you and Ray did

was low down, and you gon' have to give account …
in this life and the next."

Starting to feel the impact of her mother's words,
Emma nodded in agreement. "Yes ma'am, I'll apolo-
gize to Cassie, and yes, I'll figure out how to tell Baby
Lena who I really am."

"And that's why you and yo' sister gon' have to
come togetha'. Y'all gon' need one anotha'," E. May
said. "That li'l girl gon' have questions, and it's gon'
take both of you to answer 'em. No more secrets. No
more lies."

"What about Ray?" Emma asked.

"What about him? You get yo'self straight with yo'
child and yo' sister and let him get his self straight with
his wife and his child." As E. May spoke she realized
her words should have been uttered long ago. "You stop
worryin' about Ray Walker. That's yo' problem. He's not
yo' man; he's yo' sister's husband. Leave him alone."

Cassie woke up that morning refreshed. She hadn't
slept that soundly in a long time. Still smelling Ace's
scent on her skin, she rolled over and hugged the pillow. As the sunlight brightened her room, she closed
her eyes to see their dance one more time. It seemed

like a dream, yet it felt so real. *What would happen now? What did that dance mean to him? Would he be expecting to spend more time with me?* The reality of what could happen caused Cassie to sit up in the bed. *Am I ready for a relationship, and am I ready to share my personal baggage with someone? I'm not legally divorced from Ray.*

Cassie tried to shut down her mind and just re-member the beauty of the dance: how they moved in harmony with one another, how his arms felt holding her, the softness of his skin, the passion in his kiss.

Looking at the clock, she decided to get up and get her day started by going to the Greens' house. She knew there would be a lot to do: laundry, dishes, gro-cery shopping, and picking up Mr. Green's medicine from the pharmacist. She enjoyed her job because they were a nice couple who kept to themselves. They seemed genuinely concerned about her, but they nev-er delved into her personal life. They were educators with a nice library in their home, and they appreciat-ed Cassie's intellect and desire to read.

It was a warm fall day, so Cassie decided to put on her denim gauchos and her multicolored blouse. The blue, red, and orange in the top always looked good next to her skin. Plus, she thought, the outfit would still look good for work that night if she didn't have time to change. Completing her morning routine, she combed her hair back in a ponytail, looked at herself one last time in the mirror, and left the room. There was only one other roomer in the house besides Cassie and the owner, and she barely saw either of them. The owner was an older man who had served in the Korean War. He spent a lot of time with his family in New Orleans and traveling to Detroit trying to win his wife back. Cassie got all this information from him when she first moved in. The other roomer was a female, who appeared to be in her thirties or forties. Cassie didn't know her story. The two were cordial but not talkative. If they happened to be in the kitchen or living area at the same time, they kept their conversation generic and at a minimum. Cassie didn't mind because she had her own story she wasn't ready to share.

As she stepped outside, Cassie soaked in the fresh autumn air. She could see the neighborhood was already buzzing with people out and about enjoying their Saturday.

———◆———

"Johnny, let me borrow yo' car," said Emma, still thinking about the conversation she had with her mother earlier that day. "I wanna go to Crystal Springs."

Johnny was always working on his Buick. No one knew if something was ever really wrong with it, but he could always be found either under the hood or laying on the ground underneath it. Whatever he was doing on this particular day caused him to be more filthy than normal. His handsome face and caramel-colored skin were covered in oil and dust. Emma loved all her siblings, but she and Johnny had a special bond. Not only did they have similar outgoing personalities, but despite all that she had done he never treated her differently.

"For what?" he asked, giving her a hard time.

"That ain't none of yo' business," she shot back.

"You right. And my car ain't none of *yours*," he said sarcastically.

"Johnny, I wanna go see Bunnie. She and I ain't talked in a while, and I got a few things heavy on my mind." Bunnie was Will Lee's sister, and she and Emma had been friends since they were kids just like Ray and Will Lee had been friends.

"That's righhtt. I forgot she moved to Crystal Springs. That's why she ain't been around," he said attentively. "What time you wanna go? I might take you myself."

"Oh Lord. Please don't think you gon' go over there and try to talk to her. She ain't interested in you. As long as we been friends, she ain't neva looked yo' way, so please don't go and make a fool of yo'self. You have no have rap," she laughed.

"Li'l' sister, stay outta grown folks' business," he said.

"So, you gon' let me use the car?" Emma stood with her hand on her hip, waiting for an answer.

"Yeah, but don't stay all night. Me and Freddy goin' out tonight. We gon' hit some spot my man been talkin' about in Crystal Springs."

"And you ain't invite me? Maybe I wanna go," she pretended to pout.

"Nope. This a man's night. And definitely no baby sisters allowed. Here, you need to get goin' so you can get back," he said, tossing the keys.

"You needn't worry," she replied. "I'll be back to-night…some time."

Emma ran back in the house to freshen up and change her clothes. She was just as attractive as her older sister Cassie. They had the same skin tone and chestnut brown eyes. Yet there was a hardness to her face that Cassie didn't have.

Emma grabbed her purse from her room and headed for the front door.

"Auntie, can we ride?" said Lena, walking up behind her.

"Not this time, baby. I don't know how long I'ma be."

"Why? We ain't got nothin' to do," Lena whined.

"Ask Grandma to let you make sumthin'? You know how you like to try to cook."

"Hmm. Auntie, you pretty smart." Lena perked up. "Grandma!!! Auntie had a good idea for you!" The little girl skipped away eager to find her grandmother.

Emma went outside and got in the car. Before she could shut the door, Johnny hollered, "Take care of my baby!"

"You know I will," she said, revving the engine. As she pulled out of the yard, she hollered back, "See ya' tonight!"

Emma turned up the volume on the radio when she heard Aretha Franklin singing "Do Right Woman-Do Right Man." She was anxious to visit her friend because the two hadn't seen each other in a long time. Bunnie had moved away from their little community more than a year ago to live with her sister. As long as Emma could remember, Bunnie was the one person she could talk to about anything. When she got pregnant with Baby Lena, Bunnie was the first person she told. When she had to go to Memphis, it was Bunnie she cried to. It was the relationship Emma wished she still had with Cassie, but she felt she had ruined that chance. As she pulled up to the house, she could see Bunnie, Will Lee, and two other men on the porch.

"Hey," Emma said as she got out of the car.

"Girl, you must've flew over here," said Bunnie as Emma walked up the steps. "Emma, this my cousin Pete and his friend Sam. You remember Pete. He used to come and stay with us in the summer. Sam's family is from here, but he spent most of his life living with his father's family in Vicksburg. And I know you know that knucklehead over there," she said, pointing to Will Lee.

"Hey," said Emma as she sat on the porch swing next to Bunnie.

"Hey, is right. You lookin' good since the last time I seen you. Whatchu been up to?" said Pete.

"Nothin' much." Emma blushed. "Just livin'. Tryna' stay out of trouble."

"Trouble? So, you like trouble?" said Sam invitingly.

"Man, she taken. So, keep yo' bad rap to yo'self." Will Lee winked at Emma.

"Here we go," said Bunnie. "Emma didn't come all this way to be harassed by you jive fools. Y'all ain't got somewhere to be?"

"What could be better than sittin' in the company of two fine women?" Sam replied.

"Emma, let's go inside." Bunnie got up, dismissing the comment.

As the two were leaving, Pete spoke up. "We'll be here when you get back."

"Girl, what's goin' on?" Bunnie poured her friend a glass of iced tea before joining her at the kitchen table.

"It's Mama. She been on everybody's case about Cassie. She say it's time we make it right. Girl, I'm not ready for this. I know she right, but how can I break poor Lena's heart?"

"You knew this day was comin'. Y'all couldn't live that lie forever. And betta you tell her now than she find out from somebody else. You know how people talk." Bunnie handed Emma a napkin to wipe her tears.

"If I could take it all back, I would. Not Baby Lena but all the lies and the hurt. No child should have to live with a lie like this. Who were we really protectin' by keepin' my baby a secret?"

"You sho' can't go back in time. That's for sure. And no matter when you decide to tell Baby Lena, it's gon' hurt. Wish I could tell you what to do, but this one you gon' have to face on yo' own. You know I'ma always be here for you." Bunnie took a napkin and wiped her own tears. "I do wanna know one thing. Have you finally got that no-good Ray Walker outta yo' system?"

"I think so. I hope so. There's too much at stake for me not to. I jus' don't understand how our love could cause so much pain."

"Emma, it was wrong from the start. C'mon. Did you really expect to sleep with yo' sister's husband, get pregnant, and live like you in a fairytale?"

"Girl, I hear you. But when you in love, trouble is sumthin' you don't see until it's too late."

"Yeah. When it's too late and the damage is done. So, what's the plan? How you gon' tell Baby Lena?"

"Well, accordin' to Mama, Cassie and I gotta do it togetha'. That means Cassie and I gotta talk first, and she gotta forgive me before *she and I* can do anything togetha'."

"You right about that. When the last time you spoke to her?"

"It's been a long time. We drove to Jackson to check on her about three months ago cuz of a bad dream Mama had. I stayed in the car. Freddy got out to talk to her, but I could tell she wasn't happy to see us."

"Maybe sister to sister, she'll be different. And if Miss E. May say it needs to be done, I believe it cuz she a wise woman. Bunnie shifted in her seat. "Emma, you didn't ask me, but I'ma tell you anyway. Leave Ray alone. Look where it's gotten you. Nowhere. Girl, you too fine to be wastin' time on a dude who ain't neva put you first."

"Yeah, I know," said Emma. She agreed but was not convinced.

"Emma, I love you like a sister. It's gon' be alright. It may not look like it now, but it's gon' all work out." Changing the mood Bunnie stood up and started snapping her fingers and dancing. "Nowww, what we gettin' into tonight?"

"Girl, nothin'. I gotta get Johnny's car back to him. Him and Freddy goin' to some new club tonight."

"The one here in Crystal Springs?! That's where I wanted us to go! It's supposed to be a happenin' spot. Supposed to be run by some big shots from Chicago. And I hear they got all the latest music and the best liquor. Emma, you should go," said Bunnie, getting excited. "Supposedly that's where Sam works. He been braggin' all day about 'my boss this' and 'my boss that.' He tryna' convince Will Lee to work with him, and you know my brother. He love any jive hustle that'll make him a dollar. All the trouble he been in you'd think he'd learned by now."

"Girl," she said skeptically.

"Emma! When the last time you went out and let yo' hair down? It's time to get yo' groove on. Think about all them fine brothas who'll be there," she said, grabbing Emma's arm. "Come on. You know you wanna go."

"Alright! Let me get Johnny's car back to him. I'll meet you over there about nine o'clock."

"Okay, don't change ya' mind," Bunnie said as they headed toward the front door.

"Leavin' so soon?" said Sam.

"Yeah, gotta get back so I can meet Bunnie in Crystal Springs tonight," said Emma, shooting a look back at her friend.

"Well, I guess I'll check you later, then" he said.

"I guess so," she blushed.

CHAPTER SIX

As Cassie headed to Kat's Place, she laughed to herself about how Mr. Green had greeted her when she arrived to work. "Girl, you beamin' brighter than the sun! What's his name?"

She acted nonchalant, but she really wanted to tell him everything. She wanted to tell him about Ace, how they had met, and how they had danced the night before. "Mr. Green, it's a beautiful day" was her only response.

Beep! Beep! Beep!

As Cassie crossed the street she saw a car make a U-turn and come back toward her. It was the silver Thunderbird. As she reached the sidewalk, the car pulled up next to her.

"Hey, foxy mama. You wanna go for a ride?" It was Eddie leaning from the driver's side talking through the passenger window.

"I ain't interested." Cassie continued to walk without making eye contact.

"C'mon baby. Don't be like that," he said, driving alongside of her. "I know you ain't afraid of what Ace will say. That's my man fifty grand. We share everything. You ain't gotta worry about him."

Cassie had never gotten a good feeling from Eddie. She didn't like the way he talked to women, and there was a coldness in his eyes that made her uncomfortable. He was scary, and his smile seemed to mask a hidden agenda. She stopped and turned toward the car. "Look, you jive-a-- mother----. I told you I'm not interested." She surprised herself. She didn't curse like that under normal circumstances, but she hoped her harsh words would conceal her fear.

"Damn, baby. You ain't got to be so cold," he leered. "It's cool. You may not like me now, but you will. You can believe that."

As Eddie sped off, Cassie tried to regain her composure. She could hear her heart pounding and feel the sweat form on her temples. "What was that?" she said aloud. Cassie wondered how Ace could work with a man like Eddie. *Would he even care that Eddie had just tried to come on to me? And what did Eddie mean by they share everything?* Cassie was so distracted by her thoughts she didn't realize she had made it to her destination.

"Well, good evenin', Cinderella!" Kat said to Cassie.

"Good evenin'. And why am I Cinderella all of sudden?" she asked.

"Oh, I saw how Prince Charmin' moved in on yo' cleanin' to dance with you last night." Kat took the broom in her arms and swayed back and forth, singing, "Gee, gee, I'm soooo!"

Cassie tried not to laugh. "Okay, so you saw us dancin'. What else did you see?"

"Was there more?" Kat asked. "Shoot. I left to give y'all some privacy, but I guess I should've stayed and watched the rest of the show."

"Kat, girl! Stop!" she laughed. "What's wrong with you today?"

"Just in a good mood. Was lookin' over my books, and this place been doin' some pretty good business over the last few months. Seems my li'l arrangement with Mr. Chicago bringin' in the kinda dough I always expected to make."

"Congratulations, I think," Cassie said. "So, what does that mean?"

"Nothin. It just means for the first time in a long while, I'm gon' get dressed up, go out, and let someone serve me a drink."

"You closin' up on a Saturday night?"

"Yep. And *we* goin' out."

"*We?*"

"Yes. You and me, and I know you can dance," she teased. "So, go home and put on your baddest threads. We goin' out. Mr. Chicago keeps talkin' about this new spot he got down in Crystal Springs, and I wanna check it out. See what I might be missin'."

"Kat, I don't think it's a good idea."

"What? You don't think that fine chocolate man won't be happy to see you walk up in there? Shoot. The way y'all danced last night, he'll lose his cool when you come in the door."

"Kat, you gon' have to go by yo'self."

"Girl, I'm not takin' 'no' for an answer. Pretend you still at work. Only you won't be here, and you ain't gotta do nothin' but look cute and hold a cigarette in one hand and a drink in the other."

"Kat —"

"Go change. I'll pick you up about eight o'clock. It'll take us about an hour to get there."

"Kat, I can't go to the country. I haven't been down there in—"

"I know how long it's been, but do you really think you gon' run into yo' family at a place like that? Cassie, let's go out and have some fun for once. It's been a long time for both of us."

"I don't like this."

"Well, think about it on your way home, and I'll pick you up at eight," she said, turning Cassie around and pointing her toward the door.

As Cassie stepped onto the sidewalk, a chill ran down her back that had nothing to do with the weather. The idea of running into Eddie again scared her, and the idea of seeing Ace or someone else she knew—namely Ray, made her nervous. She and Ray had not parted on good terms, and she could only imagine how he would react if he saw her and Ace together. "Together," she said. *Will Ace and I be together tonight, or will he act differently in that crowd?* The chill that ran down her back quickly turned into a knot in her stomach.

As Cassie approached home she could see the other roomer sitting on the porch reading a book. "Hey" was all either of them said.

Once inside she found herself thinking of lies to tell Kat instead of finding something to wear. As much as she wanted to see Ace again, she didn't want it to be there.

"I'll just tell her I don't feel well," she said aloud. *I know it's a poor excuse, but I really don't feel well.*

Cassie looked at herself in the mirror and said, "What are you afraid of? You a grown woman. No one tells you what to do anymore. If you wanna go, then go. If you don't, then stay at home." The pep talked worked, and Cassie decided to step out of her comfort zone.

She looked in her closet and found her purple wrap-around dress with the three-quarter sleeves. She then searched through the closet to find her black cross strap, peep toe high heels. As she freshened up, she continued to wonder what the night would bring for her and Ace. *Will we dance all night? Will he pull me away to be alone? Or will he act too busy to notice me?* Only time would tell. As Cassie finished dressing, she noticed it was 7:57 p.m. She knew Kat would be punctual, so she hurried. But at the last minute she couldn't decide if she should wear the white flower in her hair. As she decided against it and opted for a necklace instead, she could hear a car pulling up to the house. She knew it was Kat, so she grabbed her clutch purse and headed out for the evening.

"Girl, you sho' takin' a long time gettin' ready," said Johnny as he sat impatiently on the couch waiting for his sister.

"Look, I'll be out in a minute," Emma hollered back.

"Must be sumthin' special," said Charlie, lighting his pipe. "I don't know the last time the two of you went anywhere togetha'. What's the occasion?"

"Daddy, we jus' goin to check out some new spot folks been talkin' about. They say some fellas from Chicago done brought the big city to the South."

"Yeah? Sound like a juke joint to me," he said, leaning back in his recliner. "Y'all be careful. Watch out for them cracker police out there on them roads and all that crazy mess they got goin' on in them juke joints. What they call that place, anyway?"

"Daddy, it ain't a juke joint. It's called a disco. They call it "Club 601," and you know I'ma take care of Emma." Johnny looked at his watch and shouted, "Girl, come on outta there!"

Just as he said that Emma opened the door. It had been a long time since she had fixed herself up to go anywhere. She felt uncomfortable standing there in her purple wrap-around dress with three-quarter sleeves.

"You look mighty nice, Emma," Charlie nodded in approval. He couldn't remember the last time he had seen her in a dress, and he smiled because he realized how attractive all his children were. Seeing Emma, Charlie couldn't help but think of Cassie. "Y'all be careful drivin', and Emma you watch out for them slick no-good fellas."

"Yes Daddy." Emma kissed her father on the top of his head. "Let's go, Johnny. You been screamin' at me for two hours."

"Yeah, two hours, and that's the best you could do?" he chuckled. "C'mon girl. Daddy, we'll see you later."

CHAPTER SEVEN

The music was thumping as the crowd streamed into the building. Once the site of an old bread company, Club 601 was designed to be the rural version of a Chicago disco-tech. Ace and his partners had been upgrading the barnlike structure for months. They had the inside painted, and had full-length mirrors added to the walls near the dance floor. On the opposite side, two old offices had been knocked down to add the bar area, and tile put down near the bar and sitting areas. In the middle were the tables and chairs. In the corner on the right was the DJ's area, complete with two turntables, speakers, and a microphone. And off to the left of the bar was the entrance to the kitchen. Ace and Eddie argued about serving food, and Ace won, saying that selling food would only keep people in there longer and cause them to spend more money. The upstairs was completely different. The long, narrow stairway led up to six old office spaces that had been converted into a den for high rollers looking for all types of illegal action. Leopard prints and lots of color decorated the rooms and furniture, and album covers and movie posters adorned the walls.

The neighbors, not fully aware of what would be happening inside this new business, were hesitant at first to have these strangers among them. Yet they secretly admired these Black men who seemed not to care what others, Black or White, thought about them. The locals warmed to the idea once they started benefitting from the renovations. Ace was very shrewd in his dealings, making sure the residents were hired to build and provide supplies for the project. Ace once said, "Put a little money in their pockets, and they'll love us."

To test that theory, Ace and Eddie opened Club 601 for business during the renovations for those who wanted to drink. These early patrons became regulars who provided free advertisement about the new place that was to come. Now with everything complete, word had spread throughout Simpson County and even in Jackson, and people were coming to see for themselves what these Black men from Chicago had built.

Ace had invited Kat hoping she would bring Cassie with her. He wanted to see Cassie again, but he hoped she wouldn't be turned off by seeing a full view of how he made his living.

At around 9:45 p.m., the club had begun to fill up. The fish was frying. The drinks were flowing. The music was blasting. The voices were loud, and the dance floor was packed. It was as if all the commotion had come together to make one song, and all the colorful people a beautiful tapestry.

Ace was careful not to look too flashy, so he wore his brown pants and vest with a white tapered collar shirt. He tried not to be impatient, but he couldn't help but watch the door for Cassie's arrival. When he finally spotted her, a seductive smirk came over his face. He attempted to hold quick, polite conversations with those who stopped him as he made his way through the crowd, but he eventually told the last person, "Later, brotha. We'll talk later."

As Ace approached, he put his hand on her shoulder. He was about to kiss her on the cheek when she spun around and cursed him.

"What the hell?!" said Emma.

"I'm sorry, baby! It's just...well...I thought you were someone else. I mean you look just like her," he said, shaking his head. "Do you have a sister?"

"What kind of tacky line is that?" Emma snapped.

"No jivin'. You look like someone I know," Ace said in his most alluring voice.

"Yeah, I have a sister, but I doubt you know her," she replied, softening her tone. "She wouldn't be caught in a place like this."

"Is that right?" said Ace, not sure if he should mention Cassie's name or not. He was certain they had to be related. "Look, please forgive me, and have a drink on me."

"Aren't you generous?" Emma eased closer to Ace.

"Who's this dude?" asked Johnny, walking up behind Emma.

"Oh, this is...?" said Emma, coming back to earth.

"Ace. My friends call me Ace," he said, extending his hand to Johnny. "This is my place, and I want y'all to enjoy yo'self tonight."

Johnny had always been an over-protective big brother. "Well, Ace. You can keep on movin' because whatever you sellin', we ain't buyin'. C'mon, Emma. We got a table over there with Bunnie and Will Lee."

"Will Lee? Since when you start hangin' out with him?" Emma asked Johnny. "Mr. Ace, apologies for my brotha. He's short on manners, but it was nice to meet you. I'm Emma and that's Johnny."

"The pleasure's all mine, baby," he said, still intrigued by the resemblance of the woman to Cassie.

Ace followed the movement of Emma's body as she walked away. When he turned to go back he saw Cassie and Kat come in the door. The likeness was incredible, and the fact that they were wearing the same dress made them look not like sisters—but twins.

Ace wondered what the relationship was between the two. Was this why Cassie was so secretive and guarded? Seeing her in that light, she looked even more beautiful than the night they first danced. And while she and the woman could pass for twins, there was a spark in Cassie's eyes that was uniquely hers. His desire for her was undeniable.

Making his way over to them, Ace said, "Welcome, ladies. I got to say you the two finest women in here! I'm glad you made it." Ace kissed Cassie's cheek. "And you, Miss Cassie, I've been waitin' all night for you."

"How'd you know I'd be here?" she batted her eyes.

"Because you wanted to see me as much as I wanted to see you," he grinned.

"Oh Lord, I need a drink!" said Kat, pushing past them.

"Kat, don't leave," Cassie called after her.

"Don't worry, baby. You in good hands," Ace said, bringing her in for a hug. "Let me show you around."

———————

"Grandma, these the best tea cakes ever!" said Baby Lena. "Thank you for showin' us how to make 'em."

"Alright, and don't come cryin' in the morning tellin' me yo' belly hurt," said E. May, trying to sound stern but secretly enjoying the time with the girls.

"We only ate three a piece," said Helene, licking her fingers.

"Try four or five," said E. May. "And I ain't forgot what time it is. Y'all know it's almost ten o'clock."

"Grandma, you can let us stay up. We'll be good company till Aunt Emma and Uncle Johnny come back," said Lena.

"You needn't think I'm gon' let y'all stay up till God knows when," she smiled. "They betta be glad I let them go out."

"Grandma, you was gon' make them stay in the house? Ain't they grown like you?" asked Baby Lena.

"Yeah, they grown, but they ain't like me. I'm the mama. No matter how old they get, I'ma always be older."

"You'd give my daddy a whuppin' if he did sumthin' bad?" asked Helene.

"Yes indeed. All of 'em know I'll take a switch in a minute, and they best not run or raise they hand back," she said confidently.

"Is that why my mama went away, cuz she did sumthin' bad?" asked Baby Lena.

Stunned at first, E. May replied, "Naw, baby. Yo' mama left cuz some bad things happened, and it made her upset." She wanted to say more, but instead she stood up and began putting away the dishes.

"Grandma, you think I can go see my mama one day? If she don't come home?" Baby Lena had never had the nerve to ask before, but she could tell her grandmother was in a good mood. And for some reason she felt like it would be easier if she went to see her mother than for her mother to come and see her.

"We'll see, baby," was all E. May could say. "We'll see."

———

"I thought you said Freddy was comin'," said Bunnie.

"You know how he is. One minute he's up, the next minute he's down," said Emma. "I don't even think he got outta bed today."

"You know that ni--a said he was comin' here to-night," said Will Lee to Johnny and Emma as they all sipped their drinks and waited for their fish sandwiches.

"Who?" Johnny asked.

"Ray," Will Lee replied.

"He neva was afraid of trouble," said Johnny, scanning the place. "I just hope he know what he gettin' himself into."

"How much they say he in for?" asked Emma.

"Not sure," said Will Lee. "Some say $100. Some say $500. But it ain't about the money. These city dudes don't wanna be ripped off by no country boy. It's bad for their image."

"Lawd, I hope he don't come and stir up no trouble," said Bunnie.

"Will Lee, where Pete and Sam? I was sure they would be here," said Emma.

"Oh, they here somewhere tryna' be big shots," he laughed.

"Emma, please tell me you ain't interested in that Sam," said Bunnie, knowing her friend's attraction to bad boys.

"Just curious is all." Emma tried to sound indifferent.

Over on the other side, Ace was giving Cassie the grand tour. As he led her in the direction of the stairs,

Ace spoke to all who wanted his attention. Men and women, who were familiar with his reputation, wanted to shake his hand. The men grinned widely, and the women flirted, trying to catch his eye. Some of them even made a point to give Cassie jealous glares.

"What's up here?" Cassie asked.

"My office," he said, reaching for her hand. "I figured we could get away from the noise for a li'l while."

As they reached the top of the stairs, they turned to the left and went to the last door. Cassie tried to see in the other two rooms as she passed by them, but the low lighting inside and the beads hanging in the doorways obscured her view.

"Here it is," he said, opening the door. "Take a seat anywhere your pretty heart desires."

"Thank you," she said, sitting in a chair near the desk. "This is a big place you got. Business must be good."

"We do alright," he said, taking his seat behind the desk.

"I know Kat seems to be doin' good since she started doin' business with you," Cassie said, trying to figure out why he sat so far away but feeling relieved that he did.

"I didn't wanna to scare you off," he said, sensing her body language.

"Huh?"

"You wonderin' why I sat over here, and you on the other side of the desk. I want you to be comfortable, and plus I wanna look into those beautiful brown eyes. Do you realize how fine you are? Any man would be lucky to have a good-lookin' woman like you."

Speechless, "Ohh really?" was all she could think to say.

"And I know you book smart too," he said, sitting forward. "Mmm. Mmm. Mmm. The whole package."

"How is it that you think you know so much about me?" Cassie asked, smiling and leaning closer to the desk.

"When you grow up like I did, and in my business, you gotta know how to read people. And don't forget, we shared a dance. You can learn a lot in a dance," he winked.

"Is that right? What else did that dance tell you?" she asked.

"Now Miss Cassie, would it be good for me to show all my cards?"

"Try me."

"I won't give it all, but I do know it's been a long time since you been held."

"Really?"

"Yeah, you act tough, but that's cuz you gotta be. You don't have a man like me to take care of you," he said, getting up from the desk and taking her hand. As she stood up he pulled her in and began to dance with her slowly. He whispered in her ear, "You deserve to be held and protected. You a special woman, Cassie. The brotha that let you get away must be crazy."

Cassie closed her eyes and pressed her head into Ace's chest as they danced to their own music. They found silence in each other's arms, escaping all the commotion that swirled around them. Both forgetting the parts of themselves they couldn't reveal.

CHAPTER EIGHT

On the outside there was a different type of music. The air was warm, and nature was singing its own song. Ray, who was unable to find a place to park in the front, turned down a sparse patch of land running alongside the building. He had borrowed the car from his Aunt Gee, something he often did. When he found a space near a few other cars he laughed to himself, *Nobody not from here gon' park on this little patch of dirt.* As he parked the car and turned off the engine, he sat for a while. He felt his left pocket where he had the money folded, and he felt his right side where he had the gun tucked in the waist of his pants. He wanted to pay the money he owed, but he also wanted to be prepared just in case they decided to start trouble. Ray lit a cigarette, took a couple of drags, and got out of the car. As he walked, he passed by a couple too busy whispering in each other's ears to notice him. As he got closer, he could hear Stevie Wonder's "Superstition."

"Well, whatta you know? Look who decided to show his face," said Eddie, stepping out from nowhere. "You gots to be a bold ni--a to show your face 'round here."

"Look man, I ain't come for no trouble." Ray felt the gun on his waist. "I came to pay you what I owe and call it even."

"Naw blood. It ain't that easy? I don't know how ya'll do it down here, but where I'm from you don't cheat a man and just walk away. You gots to be taught a lesson." Eddie had a viciousness in his eyes as he exposed a switchblade.

"C'mon man. It ain't gotta go down like this. I got the money right here." Ray backed up.

"Oh, I'ma cut yo' throat, then I'ma take yo' money." Eddie lunged forward to strike Ray.

As he came close, Ray squeezed the trigger on the pistol that was still concealed under his sport coat. With one *pop*, Eddie's eyes widened, and he looked at Ray in surprise. He never imagined one of those country boys would be carrying a gun. Eddie grabbed Ray's arm, trying to steady himself as he felt his body give way. Panicking, Ray shook loose from Eddie's grasp and watched him hit the ground. He looked about to see if anyone was around. Seeing no witnesses, Ray took off for his car. Sweating and breathing hard, he got in, started it up and drove off.

Eddie gasped for air as he scratched and clawed at the dirt, trying to get up. When he thought he heard voices, his motions—only in his mind—became even more erratic, but in the darkness and amid the noise no one could see or hear him.

What was only several minutes seemed liked hours, as Eddie lay there with the blood from his wound wetting the ground underneath him. He thought surely someone would be coming by soon. Try as he might, he couldn't stay awake. Taking one last shallow breath, he closed his eyes and passed out.

While Eddie lay alone on the outside, the partying on the inside continued uninterrupted. Like the rest of the crowd, Emma, Bunnie, Will Lee, and Johnny had worked up a sweat on the dance floor.

"Whew!" Emma said, falling into the chair.

"You still got it, girl," said Bunnie.

"Yeah, but I feel like I might've broke it!" Emma vigorously waved the little cocktail napkin trying to cool off.

"Y'all too much," said Will Lee. "Let me get us another round of drinks so we all can cool off."

———— ◆ ————

"Eddie, man, you out here?" called Sam. "Eddie, it's Sam. Where you at?"

"Man, maybe he still inside," said Pete.

"He told me to meet him out here. Said he had a job for me. Wanted me to watch the door," said Sam.

"Watch the door?" asked Pete.

"Yeah, supposedly there's some fool that's gon' get worked over if he come here tonight," said Sam matter-of-factly.

"And whatchu supposed to do?" Pete knew Sam was attracted to the dangerous life, but he also knew Sam wasn't a dangerous person.

"Hey man, I don't know. The brotha said be here, and I'm here."

"Look, I ain't down for all this. I'm goin' back in to sit with my family," said Pete.

"That's a sissy move," said Sam. "You ain't ready for no real work, but that's cool. You go ahead back inside to *yo' family*. I'ma be right here when Eddie comes lookin' for me. That brotha's the real deal. He got the baddest threads, the finest women, and he's makin' a lot of bread."

Sam stood at the door vigilantly waiting for Eddie unaware that he was laying a short distance away clinging to life.

———————

Ray gripped the steering wheel as he sped back to his aunt's house to drop off her vehicle. He knew it wouldn't be long before someone came looking for him. The police wouldn't care so much about some Black northern hood getting killed. It was those who worked with the man that Ray was worried about. He thought to himself, *Killed? Did I really jus' kill a man?* A lump rose up in his throat. He had done a lot of wrong in his life, but he wasn't a killer. Ray's mind was racing. *Maybe he wasn't dead. Maybe someone came out and helped him. And if someone saw him, then maybe they saw me. And if he's not dead, then I'm dead because he's going to be looking for me.* Along the way he turned off the road and headed to a nearby creek. He got out and searched the trunk until he found an old, crumpled paper bag. He wrapped up the gun and tossed it in the water. He couldn't hear the splash over the pounding of his own heart.

When Ray finally arrived at his aunt's, he sat in the car motionless, drenched in perspiration, staring out into night. He wiped his face as if trying to erase the last half hour. He opened the car door and slowly got out. As he walked to the porch, his legs and feet felt heavy. Ray hoped no one would ask him any questions. *If they ask what's wrong, I'll jus' say I drank too much.*

"Who is it?" someone called from inside.

"It's me, Ray," he hollered back. "I'm bringin' back the car."

"It's open. Come on in."

Ray tried to straighten up before opening the door. He took a deep breath and stepped inside. There in the front room, sitting in the dark, was his aunt watching a western on a small black-and-white television. Not looking up from her program, she said, "You back awful early."

"Yes ma'am. I forgot I was supposed to be at Mr. Charlie's in the morning, and I didn't wanna get too drunk and forget."

"Uh-huh," she answered still watching her show. Ray lied too easily. She knew he was probably in some kind of trouble, but she never questioned him. He was her sister's only son. She would do anything for him, but after a mild stroke she learned not to get upset every time he had a problem. She figured he would eventually learn whether the easy way or the hard way. He was in God's hands.

———

"Man, I been standin' out here a long damn time," said Sam to himself. "No Eddie. No dude with money. No one. I'm out here missin' all the action." Sam took out a cigarette and decided to take a smoke before returning inside. As he stepped off the last step and began walking toward the road, he saw a large shadowy figure on the ground. "What the hell?" Sam couldn't decide if he should continue forward or turn back. He crept toward it and realized it was a person.

"Man, you alright?" he said, bending down to help. "Eddie! Man, what happened?!" He was shocked to discover who it was.

Barely conscious, Eddie tried to speak as Sam struggled to get him turned over. That's when Sam noticed the blood covering both Eddie and the ground where he lay. "Man, Eddie, what happened to you?!" Sam took him by his shoulders and dragged him to a nearby tree to prop him up. "Man, what happened? Who shot you?" He asked anxiously. "Look, you wait here. I'ma get you some help."

Not knowing what to do, Sam went back inside and asked the bartender if he had seen Ace. Sam had never dealt directly with him, but he knew this was something Ace would want to know about right away regardless of the messenger. Sam made his way through the throngs of people to Ace's office. When he got to the door he hesitated. Realizing he was getting involved in something much more than a side hustle, he started backing away. But then he thought, *If Eddie lives he'll know I didn't get help.* Torn between two decisions, Sam stepped forward again and knocked on the door.

Inside Ace and Cassie had long since stopped dancing and were about to take their relationship to another level. The mood was interrupted by Sam's frantic knocking.

"Mr. Ace, sir. My name is Sam. I work with Eddie. He's been hurt real bad. He's outside," Sam said all in one breath.

Trying to process what he just heard, Ace buttoned his shirt and grabbed his vest. "Wait here," he said to Cassie. Shocked and scared, Cassie began pulling herself together. She didn't know if she should wait or find Kat and leave. *Eddie's been hurt. Wonder what he did. Serves that bastard right.* She couldn't help but feel Eddie got what he deserved after their brief confrontation on the street.

While Cassie contemplated her next move, Ace and two of his men followed Sam outside. When they reached the tree where Eddie was propped up, he was unconscious but still breathing.

"Eddie, man! Can you hear me?" said Ace, slapping the man's face. "What the hell happened here?"

Sam, feeling guilty for no reason, nervously tried to explain. "I waited for Eddie like he said. He said we were gonna watch the door togetha', but he neva came. So, I came outside to catch a smoke, and that's when I found him layin' here."

"Damn" was all Ace could say. "Y'all get him in his car and wait for me." Ace was conflicted. He knew Eddie was a snake, and if the roles were reversed Eddie would probably let him die. He also thought how running things would be a lot smoother without Eddie. "Was anybody else around?" Ace asked Sam.

"Can't say for sure, but I don't think so." Sam stood there biting his bottom lip as he often did when he was in trouble.

"Look, you know any Black doctors around here?" Ace bent down to take another look at Eddie.

"Yeah, but there's also a hospital not too far," Sam responded.

"Can't risk it. We take Eddie to a hospital, the cops will be snoopin' around by daylight," said Ace.

"We can try Dr. Waters. He a fair man, and a good doctor. He won't ask too many questions," said Sam.

"Good. You three take Eddie to that doctor. I'll stay here, keep things cool, and see if I can get the lowdown on what happened. I'll be waitin' for an update. Use the phone in the car. And Stan, if you do a good job with this, I might be able to find a place for you workin' directly for me."

"It's Sam, Mr. Ace. And thank you, sir." Sam felt a rush of dread and excitement.

"Okay, Sam," he replied, amused by the young man's nervousness.

Ace composed himself and went back inside. He would let fate take over now. *If Eddie lived, he lived. If he didn't, then....* Ace's only interest was returning to Cassie, but when he got back to his office, she was gone.

Downstairs, Cassie had finally found Kat and convinced her it was time to leave. The two stopped in the ladies' room before getting back on the road. "You sure you ready to go?" asked Kat. "I mean if I had some sexy Black man following after me, I just might wanna stay a li'l longer."

"Kat, it's time to go," Cassie said, convincing herself.

"Well, at least let me get one of them fish sandwiches for the road," she said.

"Alright, come on. But don't take all day," Cassie replied.

As they walked out of the bathroom, a nice-looking man staggered over to Cassie and said, "Hey foxy lady! You said we could go another round on the dance floor. You ain't tryna' stand me up are you?"

"Stand you up? Do I know you?" She knew the man was mistaken.

"Ah wow. You don't know me now," he said with a drunken slur. "That's cool, baby. You chicks is all the same." He shook his head in disbelief as he stumbled into the bathroom.

"What was that?" Cassie laughed.

"I don't know, but you didn't have to do the poor brotha like that," Kat laughed. "He so smashed we all look alike to him."

"Now I know it's time to go," Cassie said. "You hurry up. I'll be out front." Cassie headed for the exit, and Kat headed for the bar to order a sandwich.

"You were tryna' leave without sayin' goodbye?" a voice whispered in Cassie's ear. She turned to see Ace standing behind her.

"You got a lot goin' on. I don't wanna keep you from yo' work," she said, avoiding eye contact.

"Now what could I have to do that's more important than this?" he said, trying to hug her.

"Ace, it's been nice, real nice. But we're gonna have to head back home."

"Baby, what's wrong?" he asked, gently moving her face toward his.

"Ace, somebody that works for you got hurt tonight," she said. "That's too heavy for me to deal with."

"What I do?" He laughed cautiously. "Look baby, don't leave like this. At least talk to me. Tell me to go to hell or sumthin'. Don't just walk out."

"It's late," she said, looking away. "And we gotta get on the road. I'll see ya later."

Ace watched her walk out the door. He didn't know if he should go after her and risk a scene or let her cool off and talk to her later. He chose the latter.

Cassie went outside and breathed a sigh of relief. A thousand questions went through her mind. *Who hurt Eddie? What if they wanted to hurt Ace too? What if me and Ace had been outside? Who was that crazy man who thought I owed him a dance?* Feeling exhausted from the evening, Cassie braced herself against the wall, closed her eyes, and waited for Kat.

Inside, Ace, feeling rejected, made his way through the crowd to find Emma's table. "You havin' a good time, pretty lady?" he asked, ignoring everyone else.

"Everythang been real nice," she said, wiping the sweat from her face. "The music, the food, it's all been good."

"Glad y'all could come and check us out," said Ace, finally acknowledging the others at the table.

"Yeah, been real nice," said Johnny as he got up. "Hate we gotta be leavin'."

"Wait, now," said Ace. "Can a brotha get at least one dance?"

"Naw," said Johnny abruptly. "C'mon Emma."

"Johnny!" said Emma. "It's one dance."

Ace took Emma's hand and led her to the dance floor. As they made their way, he shot a look to the DJ, and the music slowed down. Ace moved her in close as they started to dance. He closed his eyes and imagined he was dancing with Cassie. The thought of Cassie made Ace hold Emma a little tighter. Emma, unaware, nestled into Ace's arms as their bodies moved in harmony to George Benson's "Masquerade". When the song ended Emma whispered "thank you" as she pulled away.

"Don't go yet, Ca—," he whispered, pulling her back and almost saying Cassie's name.

"Whatchu say?" Emma jerked away and looked at Ace.

"I said 'don't go yet.'"

"No. It sounded like you were getting ready to say something else." Emma's voice was getting louder.

"Look baby, c'mon. Don't get worked up," he said, trying to avoid a scene. "Do you know how many chicks I've danced with tonight? I'm sorry for messin' up yo' name."

"No. But it sounded like you were going to call me 'Cassie'," she said unsure of herself.

"So, what of it?" he said, feeling confident he had fixed his mistake. "Would you like it betta if I had called you a different wrong name? Denise? Barbara?"

"That's crazy," she said, ignoring his question. "Look, thank you for the dance, but I gotta get back to my brotha. It's been nice."

"My pleasure, baby," he said, kissing her hand. "Maybe we can do it again sometime."

"Maybe," she said, smiling but still unaware of what had just transpired.

As Emma walked backed to the table, Kat was making her way outside with her fish sandwich in its greasy brown bag. "You ready, girl?" she said, seeing Cassie resting against the wall.

"Yeah," she said. "It's been a helluva night. Don't know the next time I'll let you talk me into this."

"Ah girl. You know you had a good time," Kat responded.

As they made their way to the car, Cassie noticed the wet, stained ground near the base of one of the trees. She immediately thought about Eddie. "I can't wait to get home," she sighed.

CHAPTER NINE

Dr. Waters continued to shake his head as he examined the bullet hole. He knew even if he were able to remove it, the chances of Eddie surviving could be slim. He went to his cabinet and pulled out a needle and a small vial. "You'll thank me later," he said as he stuck the needle in Eddie's left arm. Eddie felt his heartbeat slow down and his breathing lighten up. He let go and surrendered to the sleep. Dr. Waters moved around with ease and focus as he collected his instruments.

Outside, Sam and the other two men waited in silence, each smoking a cigarette. No one talked, but everyone was thinking the same thing: *What happens if Eddie dies?* Finally, Sam broke the silence. "Think we should call Ace and give him the news?"

"What news?" said the one who drove them there. "Just be cool. We'll call when that doctor come out and tell us if Eddie dead or alive."

A couple of hours had gone by, and Dr. Waters had successfully removed the bullet from Eddie's side. He thought to himself how different the outcome might have been if Eddie had been shot in the stomach like the men said. He stitched up the opening and covered it with gauze. What Dr. Waters was really worried about was the amount of blood Eddie had lost. He wanted to recommend again that they take Eddie to the hospital, but he had a feeling these weren't the type of men who took advice. So, he did as he was asked and kept quiet.

———————

"You were awfully quiet the whole way home," said Kat, pulling up to Cassie's house. "Girl, what's goin' on?"

"Don't even know where to start," Cassie said, slumping back in the seat instead of getting out. "If I told you I'd probably have to kill you."

"Girl, you crazy. Yo' problem is you lookin' for love instead of reality."

"What?" Cassie looked at Kat confused.

"You know what kind of man Ace is," she answered softly. "You know what he does. Hell, it didn't take me long to figure out the brotha wasn't tellin' me the whole story, but I made a choice. The money is good. I keep my distance and act ignorant. If you want him, you have to make a choice. Either you accept him and what he does, or you let him go."

"Is it worth it, though?" Cassie questioned herself.

"Cassie, I know all of this could end tomorrow. Ace and his buddies could skip town. They could get busted or worse. I'm prepared for that. That's reality."

"You right, Kat. I gotta figure out what I'ma do. I knew not to go down this road in the first place, but here I am. And I sho' ain't gon' have no answers tonight, so what I'ma do is go inside and get ready for bed. It's been a *long* day."

"Don't forget *fun*," Kat teased.

"Yeah, lots of fun. Good night, girl."

Cassie opened the door to the house, and then closed it like she was securely shutting out all the drama she had seen and felt that day. As she got ready for bed, she caught a whiff of Ace's cologne in her clothes. "What have I gotten myself into," she said as she tossed the dress into the hamper. Cassie put on her nightgown, took her hair down, and climbed into bed. She was determined to get a good night's rest, so before she went to sleep she closed her eyes and said her prayers.

"Gentlemen, I'm all finished," said Dr. Waters, standing at the door. "Your friend is sleeping. I removed the bullet, but he lost a lot of blood. He needs to go to a hospital. I'll let him sleep and watch him for thirty more minutes to see how he does, then you can take him."

"Thanks Doc," they all said in their own way.

"Okay genius, now we call Ace," the driver said to Sam.

All three walked to the car, and the driver called Ace. "Yeah. He alive. The doctor said he removed the bullet from his side. Yeah. The doctor said he should go to the hospital. Naw. You wanna us to bring him there, or take him to the hospital? Alright. Cool."

"So, now what?" Sam asked, trying not to sound worried.

"We drop him off," said the driver, taking another drag of his cigarette before tossing it on the ground.

"We takin' him to the hospital?" Sam asked.

"Look man, you just sit tight. Let the grownups handle this. I don't know why Ace sent you out here anyway," he said, getting frustrated.

Not wanting to sound weak, Sam snapped back, "So I could show yo' a-- how to get here."

The second man, who hadn't said anything, let out a laugh that stunned them all. His laughter cut the tension, and soon everyone was laughing.

"We gotta do this more often," Emma said to Bunnie as they all walked to their cars.

"Yeah, it's been too long," said Bunnie. "I had a good time with you nuts."

"I'm just glad Ray decided not show," said Johnny.

"Yeah man. That could've been some real heavy sh-t," said Will Lee. "And where is Sam? I ain't seen him all night."

"Hell if I know. Somewhere tryna' be a gangsta," Pete said unconcerned.

"Alright girl, we'll talk," said Bunnie.

"Good night, y'all," said Johnny.

The ladies hugged; the men shook hands. As Johnny and Emma rode home, they joked about the events of the night.

"I wish Cassie and Freddy had been there," Johnny lamented. "Don't know the last time we all was togetha'."

"That would've been sumthin'." Emma smiled. "Can't you just see Cassie with her prim and proper self on the dance floor?"

"*That* would've been sumthin'," he chuckled. "She ain't neva had no rhythm."

———————

The men rode away from Dr. Waters' place as discreetly as they had come there. In the dark night the only sounds to be heard were the crushing of gravel under the car tires and the cool wind blowing through the open windows. No one said a word, and at some point not even the radio could be heard.

As the air blew through the car, Eddie struggled to wake up. He didn't who he was with or where he was. It seemed the more he struggled to move the more pain he felt. Eddie, thinking he was asking, "Where are we going?" was only being heard in the moans and groans of his discomfort.

"Man, can you drive a little faster? This dude is lookin' real bad," said Sam.

Watching Eddie lay helpless, covered in blood and sweat, Sam thought about his own life and the direction it was headed. He remembered how intimidated and intrigued he was when he first met Eddie.

Sam wanted that type of power and respect but seeing Eddie there powerless and weak made him wonder if the pursuit was worth it.

The men arrived back at Club 601 hours later.
Most of the crowd was gone. Only a few people remained at the bar.

"Hey, I need to see you." Ray whispered into the
phone.

"Tonight? It's late. What's wrong? Why you
talkin' so low?" Emma stood in the kitchen in her
night gown and hair rollers; she had gotten up for a
glass of water. "You know you woke the whole house
callin' this late. What's goin' on?"

"Look, I done got into some trouble, and I gotta
get out of town."

"What else is new," she said, rolling her eyes. She
had heard this script before. Irritated but concerned
she asked, "Whatchu do this time?"

"I can't talk about it now. I just wanna see you
before I go. I'll be around there about four o'clock."

"Okay, be careful.".

As Emma returned to her room she heard her
father's voice. "What he do now?"

"Daddy, you know Ray. It could be anything," she said, making light of it but feeling this time it was something more serious.

Emma tossed and turned, waiting for Ray to knock on the window. She wanted to know what was going on. Assuming she had more time before he arrived, Emma found that right spot on the pillow and drifted off to sleep.

"Emma. Emma. Wake up," said Ray, gently shaking her.

"Ray, you alright?" she said startled. "What's goin' on?"

"I can't get into it, and the less you know the betta." Ray sat on the bed beside her. "I'ma have to get away for a while."

"Ray, when you gon' stop this? You have a child to think about." Emma tried not to raise her voice.

"I know baby, but believe me, this time I didn't go lookin' for trouble. Trouble came lookin' for me." He wanted to tell Emma everything. How he'd gone to the club to pay the money he owed, and how he'd shot and killed a man in self-defense.

"Look, do what you gotta do. Just be careful." Emma kissed him. "And call me when you safe."

"I'ma get over to the bus station and catch the first thing out. Baby don't worry. You know I always land on my feet," he said, trying to ease both their fears. Ray kissed Emma's forehead before heading back out the window.

Emma slid back underneath the covers and pulled them over her head so no one could hear her cry.

———

"Alright big man. You go inside and tell Ace we here with the package," the driver said to Sam.

Sam looked at Eddie and got out of the car to do as he was told. When he got inside he surveyed the entire area before spotting Ace upstairs. Their eyes met and Ace nodded, acknowledging Sam. Ace went inside his office for a few minutes before coming downstairs to meet Sam. "Let's go," said Ace.

The driver and the passenger were standing next to the vehicle while Eddie lay slumped in the back seat. "Alright fellas. I'll take it from here," said Ace. "You boys go in and close the place up. Make sure them fools don't try to rip me off. And Stan, you can split."

Without any formal goodbyes, the men went their separate ways. The driver and the passenger went inside the club. Sam headed up the road, and Ace got inside the car with Eddie.

Ray tried not to look suspicious or draw attention to himself as he waited for the bus. He would have to travel to Jackson to catch the bus to Memphis. There were only a few people in the station besides the White manager. There was an older White couple and one Black man who appeared to be around the same age as Ray. With the extra change in his pocket, Ray bought himself a cool drink from the machine and found a seat in the corner away from everyone. He knew the next bus wouldn't leave until 7:00 a.m., so he tried to relax. But each time he closed his eyes he replayed the moment he pulled the trigger. Ray wondered if the man was dead or alive, and he tried to convince himself it wasn't his fault. *I wasn't looking for trouble. I went there to settle a debt. If he's dead then it's his fault.* Deep down Ray was remorseful, and he hoped he hadn't killed him.

CHAPTER TEN

"They say it's some uppity-looking Black fellow. Shame to be left to die like that," said the bus station manager to one of the drivers as they stood at the counter drinking coffee. Ray tried to listen without being obvious. Why had this conversation awakened him? He didn't realize he'd been napping for almost four hours. By this time a bus had arrived and the station was bustling with activity.

"Sheriff say from the way he was dressed, he definitely wasn't from around these parts. No I.D. and no witnesses." Ray sat up in his seat. *Was that the man from last night? If he was dead who moved his body?* Ray didn't know if he should feel sick at the idea that he might have killed someone or relieved that there was no evidence of a crime.

"Seven o'clock bus to Jackson now boarding," Ray heard the station manager say over the intercom. Ray sat frozen. He didn't know if he should board the bus or stick around to learn the identity of the slain Black man.

"Seven o'clock bus to Jackson now boarding."

———

Cassie awoke the next morning around 8:30 a.m. to a knock on her bedroom door. "Hey, phone for you," said her housemate.

"Okay." Cassie rubbed the sleep from her eyes.

"Hello," she said in her raspy morning voice.

"Good mornin'," said the voice on the other end.

"Good mornin', Ace," she said, quickly clearing her throat.

"We didn't end the night right, so I had to call," he said. "I can't have you mad at me."

Cassie was flattered, worried, and excited, but all she could say was, "How'd you get my number?" Before Ace could answer, Cassie answered her own question. "Kat."

"Yes ma'am. It was hard convincin' her not to stand in the way of true love," Ace laughed. "I don't think she like me."

Cassie couldn't help but laugh. "Kat don't like too many people. Sometimes I wonder if she like me."

"Baby, I can't imagine who wouldn't like you," Ace said.

"You'd be surprised," she said flatly. "Ace, thank you for callin', but I don't wanna waste your time. You got a lot going on."

"Pretty lady, you could neva waste my time. You could break my heart but neva waste my time. Jus' say you'll let me take you out. You and me alone. If you still feel the same after our date, I'll leave you alone."

Cassie did want to see him again, and they hadn't had an opportunity to spend time alone. "Okay," she said.

"Far out, baby. I'll pick you up at three o'clock."

"Okay," she said. "I'll meet you at Kat's."

"You don't want me to know where you stay. That's cool," he said. "I'll pick you up from there. Three o'clock."

"Three o'clock."

Cassie whirled her way back to her room with a wide grin across her face. It had been a long time since a man had made her feel that way. Ace hadn't shared where they were going, so she had no idea what to wear. It didn't matter what they did, because she was looking forward to being with Ace away from work just the two of them. Cassie stood at her closet and finally decided on a pair of jeans, a light sweater, and her tennis shoes.

At about 2:30 p.m. Cassie walked outside into the Sunday afternoon sun. Strolling along, she thought about Baby Lena and how big she must have gotten since the last time she saw her. She pictured Lena in her church dress and her mama singing in the choir. Cassie really missed her family. She didn't miss the hurt and pain she'd experienced, but she longed for the love and togetherness she knew growing up. She laughed to herself as she thought about how different everything was from the way it used to be before the betrayal.

As she arrived at Kat's, she saw a light on and decided to knock. Kat came to the door dressed as if she had been cleaning all day

"Whatchu doin' here?" Kat examined her friend from head to toe.

"What kinda welcome is that?" Cassie said, walking inside.

"Girl, I'm sorry. I just ain't used to you being here this time of day unless you sleepin' off the night before," she joked.

"You ain't right," Cassie chuckled.

"But seriously, why you here?" Kat said, taking a seat.

"I got a date," she said nonchalantly.

"Well alright!" Kat responded. "Mr. Chicago, I presume?"

"Yes, and I told him to pick me up here," she said.

"Where y'all goin'?"

"I'm not sure. That's why I didn't know what to put on."

"I don't think he'll care," said Kat, pointing to the window. Ace had arrived in a blue Monte Carlo.

Cassie's face instantly lit up with excitement. She said a hurried goodbye and went outside. Seeing Cassie, Ace got out of the car and greeted her with a hug. "Hey pretty lady."

"Hey yourself," she said, waiting for him to open the door. "I hope I'm dressed okay. You didn't tell me where we were goin'."

"Baby, you look just fine. Trust me," he said as they both waved to Kat.

"So where *are* we goin'?" Cassie stared at Ace, admiring how gorgeous he looked in his jeans and t-shirt.

"Well, I thought we might drive to New Orleans and kick up our heels," he said, kissing her hand.

"What? Ace, I'm not dressed for a trip to New Orleans," she said.

"Relax, I'm just jivin'," he laughed. "Today is our day. We gon' kick back and enjoy each other outside in God's creation."

After driving for about forty minutes, Ace made a turn down a small, dusty road. After about ten more minutes the vehicle slowed, and Ace parked near an open space of trees. "Come on." He got out and pulled a big brown grocery bag from the back seat. "Baby, I'm takin' you on a picnic."

Trying to contain her happiness, Cassie said, "Okay. Let's do it."

"Here, take this." He handed her a neatly folded red blanket. "Follow me."

As they made their way through the trees, they came upon a beautiful lake. Cassie beamed with joy as she saw the sunlight sparkle off the water. *How had she not known about this place? And how did Ace find it?* They located a clear area close to the lake's edge and set the blanket down. Ace took his time, proudly taking out the contents of the bag. This impressed Cassie, and she saw a gentler side of him that made him even more attractive.

Setting up everything for the two of them gave Ace a sense of relaxation and peace he rarely felt. He longed to be with Cassie away from the chaos and confusion of his work. She was a calming force, and he wanted to spend as much time with her as possible.

"You came prepared," she said as he laid out the soda bottles, sandwiches, potato chips, pickles, and napkins. "What's that for?" she asked, pointing at an apple.

"Oh, I figured we needed a fruit or a vegetable," he said jokingly.

For the next several hours Cassie and Ace talked, laughed, and ate, only occasionally stopping to notice those who passed them. They talked about music, movies, politics, their likes and dislikes, and their goals. But for all the conversation, neither of them talked about family or ventured to ask anything too personal. That is, until Cassie spoke up. "Ace, is Eddie okay?"

Completely caught off guard, Ace looked at Cassie as he searched for a response. "Ah, yeah. Everything's cool. Don't you go worryin' yo' pretty little head about that."

"I'm sorry. I didn't mean to go there," she said, hearing an awkwardness in his voice. "It's jus' I ain't neva been around nothin' like that before."

"It's cool, baby," he said, switching the subject. "Hey, let's take a walk so I can hold your hand."

Cassie agreed, and Ace stood and extended his hand to help her up. He gave Cassie that reassuring grin she loved so much as he led her toward a nearby trail.

"You know a lot about nature for a city boy," Cassie teased.

"I'm what you call a Renaissance man," he winked. "And plus, what Black man in Chicago ain't neva had to spend the summer in the South?"

They both laughed, and Ace held Cassie's hand tightly as they walked. He wanted to know more about this woman. *Where had she come from, and why was she living away from her family?* And he wanted to share details about himself. He knew in his line of work it wasn't a good idea to get too personal, but he genuinely liked Cassie and wanted her to like him. He wanted to tell her about his childhood. How his mother was only eighteen years old when she had him. How he had only met his father three times in his life, and how he wished he had a closer relationship with his sisters. For some reason he knew she could relate to the pain he had experienced. Yet, Ace said nothing, and Cassie offered no information about herself. They both kept the conversation light, enjoying the time away from their individual realities. Cassie wished the day would never end.

No matter how much they talked and laughed, Cassie did notice how Ace disconnected from their conversation a few times. He would have a distant look in his eyes, and as soon as she mentioned it, he would snap back. She didn't know where his mind was going, and she made no attempts to pry.

After about an hour, they decided to head back to where they had left their blanket. As they folded it together, Ace showed his playful side by initiating tug of war. Knowing he could overpower Cassie, he tugged the blanket just enough to pull her into his arms for a kiss. It wasn't a passionate kiss like the night before in his office. This was special; it was a sweet gesture of appreciation and acknowledgment.

The ride back was quiet, as they both wondered to themselves what would become of their relationship. Ace focused on the road while Cassie stared out the window. He had offered to drop her off at home, but she declined. As he pulled up to Kat's, Cassie began collecting her belongings and herself. She was nervous, just like the first time they had met. She didn't know what he would say, what she would say, or what they would do next. It became a lot to process. Cassie wanted to give in to her feelings for Ace and explore where their connection could go. But the reality was she was still married to Ray, and she couldn't ignore how Ace made his living.

"Ace, I really enjoyed this," she said. "I saw a whole 'nother side of you today."

"See baby I'm not the big bad wolf. I'm really just a gentle pussycat," he said, stroking her arm. "And bein' around you got a brother feelin' all sensitive."

Surprising herself, Cassie moved over and kissed Ace. "I can't wait to see you again," she said, getting out of the car before he could respond. As Ace drove away, Cassie stood there trying to decide if she should go inside the bar and share the details of her date. Seeing no sign of her friend, she headed home. Along the way she stopped by the corner market to grab some groceries for dinner. Sitting down to a nice meal would be the perfect ending to her date with Ace. She hoped her housemate was gone, so she could have the kitchen to herself.

The thought of cooking made her think about home and what she was missing. She remembered E. May's Sunday dinners, and her mother's salmon cakes were always her favorite. Cassie envisioned all the family gathered around the table. After having had seconds and thirds, they were now looking for dessert. E. May would probably serve her famous sweet potato pie.

Cassie arrived back at her place to find her housemate sitting on the couch reading *JET*. She said a quick "hello" as she passed through. Cassie set her groceries down on the kitchen counter and went to change her clothes. She was grateful to have a quiet ending to a tranquil and exhilarating day.

"Look man, I told you what I know," Ace said, trying to sound concerned. "Yeah. It's handled." Ace hung up the phone and took a deep breath. Making Eddie disappear wasn't as easy as he had expected. He would have to give more thought to the details. He would also have to make sure none of the other guys said anything. He wasn't concerned about his boys, but he didn't know enough about the new guy Sam to trust his silence. Ace was also worried about his boss in Chicago receiving information that could cast doubt on his version of Eddie's disappearance.

Ace had also started to reexamine his role in Eddie's death. A part of him felt like he should have taken Eddie to the hospital. The other part of him remembered who Eddie was and all that he'd done to try to sabotage Ace's authority, both in Chicago and in Mississippi. Eddie was dangerous and conniving. The side meetings he held with some of the workers. The private deals he had set up with some of their partners. And his rush to call Chicago every time he thought Ace wasn't conducting business the "right" way. Ace believed all of it was more than enough to justify what he did.

Ace chuckled when he thought about how Kat was one of the few business owners who had not been intimidated by Eddie, and Eddie knew it. Eddie didn't like Kat or Cassie, and he made sure Ace knew it every chance he got. Ace never reacted to Eddie's disrespectful comments about the ladies, but deep down it infuriated him. He cared about them. For the first time in years, Ace had allowed himself to get close to someone, and that scared him. How Cassie would react if she knew what he had done was something he didn't want to think about.

While Ace revisited his actions, miles away Eddie's unidentified body lay at one of the Black funeral homes. The owner wrote down "person unknown" on his intake log, and with no identification he knew there would be no next of kin to notify and no service to conduct. He had the mortician prepare the body for burial.

—◆—

Ray arrived in Memphis about noon. He bought himself a sandwich and sat in the bus station trying to decide what he should do. There were several people he could call: his sister, Matty; Cassie's Aunt

Peggie; his cousin, Verda; or his old girlfriend, Alise. Dropping in on any one of them would probably raise their suspicions, but only one of them wouldn't ask a lot of questions. And Ray could not withstand an interrogation because answers were something he didn't have. He still didn't know exactly what he was running from or why. Ray finished his sandwich and headed toward the pay phone.

"Hey Aunt Peggie. How you feelin'? Oh yeah? Me? I'm alright. Just got off the bus here and was hopin' I could stop by and see you. No ma'am. Yes ma'am. I sho' would. Yes ma'am. No trouble at all. Okay, see you soon. Thank you, Aunt Peggie."

Ray hung up the phone feeling relieved. He was glad he had called her. She was always there for the family. Her home was the safe place her nieces and nephews fled to when they needed to get away, and she treated Ray just like a blood relative. Ray understood more clearly now why E. May sent Cassie and Emma there when Emma got pregnant. Then he caught himself. He hadn't thought about Baby Lena's birth in a long time. He hoped Cassie was okay. He truly loved her, but he had allowed his affair with Emma to get out of control. Truth was, he didn't think he was worthy of Cassie's forgiveness.

He was ashamed of the decisions he had made, especially how they affected her and Baby Lena. He would go to his grave regretting the secret and lies his daughter was born into.

PART III

CHAPTER ELEVEN

The Christmas season was always a festive time for the family, and E. May made sure to cook everyone's favorite foods: chitlins for Charlie, chicken and dumplings for Johnny, fried chicken for Freddy, turnip greens for Emma, sweet potato pie for Helene, pound cake for Baby Lena, and a peach cobbler for Cassie even though she wasn't there. They weren't big on giving gifts, but they made sure to decorate the house inside and out, put up a tree, and buy presents for the girls. Charlie enjoyed going out to find a tree for Christmas. He didn't hunt anymore, so this gave him an opportunity to go out into the woods. The rest of the family enjoyed the holiday through Baby Lena's and Helene's excitement.

While all the preparations were being made, E. May was secretly praying this would be the Christmas

Cassie came home. She had no idea that miles away, Cassie was praying for the same thing.

It had been months since Cassie and Ace had their meaningful date at the lake. Since then they had continued to see each other. While their feelings for one another were obvious, they both did what they could to suppress them, each still holding onto a secret that could not be shared. They discussed spending Christmas together, but Ace had mentioned he might have to travel back to Chicago.

Since leaving home Cassie had spent the holidays with Kat. If they didn't go to Kat's cousins for dinner, then the two of them would spend the day together cooking, listening to music, and playing cards. She had enjoyed this Thanksgiving, and it almost felt like home with Ace being there. He got along well with Kat's family, who found him charming and humorous. Seeing him interact with everyone, Cassie found herself imagining that she and Ace were married and that they were sitting there with their own family. What should have been a comforting thought became a harsh reminder of how much she missed her real family. The longing Cassie felt was intensifying. She so wanted to be at home with Baby Lena, her parents, and everyone else. She just didn't know how to make amends. She had been gone three years, and it seemed like a lifetime. Not since her brothers and sister had stopped her on the street had she communicated with anyone from her family. She missed them, but she still hadn't decided when and if she would call.

Later in the day Cassie got up the nerve to phone her mother. She was afraid, but her homesickness was much stronger than any fear she had.

"Hello," said the sweet, cheerful voice on the other end.

"Hey Mama. It's me, Cassie," she said hesitantly.

"Lawd! Cassie! Baby, I knew you would call," E. May said. "You alright? When you comin' home?"

"Yes ma'am, I'm alright." She held back tears hearing the familiar sound of love in her mother's voice. "I was thinkin' maybe I would come home for Christmas."

"Oh Cassie. That would be fine. Just fine indeed," E. May said. "Yo' daddy will be so happy. And yo' brothers and sister, oh and Baby Lena. They all gon' be so excited! You need someone to come and getchu'?"

"No ma'am. I think I'll be fine gettin' there," she said. "I'll let you know if I need a ride."

"Cassie, you made my day. You doin' alright?"

"Yes ma'am. Everything is fine. I miss y'all though. How's Baby Lena?"

"Chile, we sho' miss you too," said E. May. "And that girl is sumthin'. She a smart one for sure.

"Cassie, I know you didn't call to hear this, but I gotta say it. We been doin' a lot of talkin' about what happened to you, and it was wrong. Baby, I'm so sorry you felt you had to run away."

Cassie was stunned by her mother's admission. It was the first time anyone in her family had acknowledged her mistreatment. She didn't know how to respond. "Mama, thank you. That means a lot."

"The Lawd is so good. Yes indeed. He sho' know when to show up." E. May began rocking back and forth as she often did in church when she got excited. "I think you might be my surprise present to the family."

"Mama, I don't want no big to-do," Cassie responded nervously.

"Chile, yo' mama know," she said calming down. "I'm jus' so glad to hear yo' voice and to know I'll be seein' my baby soon."

"Mama, I love you, and I look forward to seein' you too," Cassie said. "I'll call you again."

"Yes, baby. Please do," E. May said relieved. "Be sho' to let us know if you need a ride. You take care now. Love you too."

They both hung up feeling like years of hurt had been lifted from their shoulders. Cassie returned to her room, thinking *That conversation was much easier than I expected it would be.* She was glad she took that step, but she was still nervous because she knew there was more work to be done. Forgiving her mother was easy. It was the rest of her family that was going to be the challenge, particularly Emma. *How do you forgive the ultimate betrayal? Emma and Ray's affair put a hole in my heart. It's healing, but it will never be the same. Nothing will ever be the same. My life, Ray's and Emma's lives, and Baby Lena's life are bound together by a lie wrapped so tight it has strangled the entire family. Could the truth really be strong enough to restore what has been lost?* The more Cassie thought about how Baby Lena's life was going to be turned upside down by the truth, the more she reconsidered her trip home. *How do you tell a child that the mother she's always known is not her real mother?* A wave of uncertainty washed over her.

"Phone for you, Cassie!" her housemate hollered. "Cassie, phone!"

"Coming!" she hollered back.

Having just finished talking to E. May, Cassie wondered who could be calling her. "Hello?" she said.

"Baby, you were on my mind, and I had to hear your voice," said Ace on the other end. "I hope I didn't disturb you."

"Oh no, Ace. It's good to hear from you," she replied. "Whatchu doin'?"

"Baby, sittin' here contemplatin' the meanin' of life," he said jokingly. "I mean, what's life without you in it?"

"That's real heavy stuff," she laughed. "What's that, Shakespeare?"

"*Voulez vous coucher avec moi, ce soir,*" he replied. "Baby, I know Shakespeare and French. A man of many talents."

"No, you a comedian without a stage," she said, enjoying the humor. "It's a good thing I like to laugh, and I know who LaBelle is."

"So, what's happenin' today, pretty lady?" he asked.

"I just got off the phone with my mama." Cassie sounded serious.

"Everything alright?" He was concerned. This was the first time Cassie had mentioned her family, yet he didn't want to press her.

"Yeah. I called to tell her I would be home for Christmas," she responded, not knowing how much she was ready to share.

"Home for the holiday. I can dig it," he said. "Been thinkin' about my own plans for Christmas. I would love to meet yo' family."

Cassie was caught off guard by the suggestion of Ace meeting her family. "Wow. I don't know what to say," she responded. "Spendin' Christmas togetha' would be nice though."

She was flattered by the thought, but she didn't believe it was the right time or under the right circumstances. There was still a lot of tension within her family, and she didn't want Ace exposed to all of that. She also didn't want to run the risk of Ray and Ace accidentally meeting.

While Cassie pondered if Ace should be included in her Christmas plans, Ace had his own reasons for considering where he would spend the holiday. The issue of Eddie's disappearance had not gone away as quickly as he had expected. A Black man disappearing in Mississippi wasn't unusual, nor was it for men in his line of work, but Double T had been asking questions. Ace fabricated a story, telling Double T that Eddie had come to him saying he had a run-in with a Black police officer, and he'd been threatened. Eddie was hell-bent on getting revenge, and when Ace recommended Eddie play it cool so as not to bring attention to them, Eddie cussed him. He thought it was strange when Eddie didn't show up for the opening of the club, and he knew something was wrong when Eddie didn't show up at their office the next day. Ace figured Eddie's constant criticism of him would support his explanation.

Eddie felt Ace had gone soft, and Ace knew what that meant. The only thing worse than being weak was being disloyal, and both could get you killed. Ace figured after Eddie's death he would stay down South, keep a low profile, and make a substantial profit for his boss. As long as the money continued to roll in, Ace assumed Double T would be satisfied and ask no questions. He was wrong.

Ace had to ask himself if he had really become soft. Having met Cassie, he had begun to question his life and how long he would remain in the game. He hadn't done this type of self-examination since his mother died five years earlier. *What kind of future can I have as a single man, no wife and no family?* There was a part of him that wanted to go legit, but there was the other part of him—the familiar part—that didn't know what legit would even mean. *Could the love for this woman be enough for me to give up the only life I've ever known?*

"I'll let you know, Ace," Cassie said, interrupting his introspection. "It's been three years since I been home, and I don't know if this the right time to bring guests."

"Okay baby. No pressure," he replied.

"It's not that I don't wanna spend time with you," she began to explain.

"Baby, it's cool," he said. "We can work sumthin' out. We got time. The main thing is, when will I see you again?"

All afternoon E. May found it hard to contain her emotion. Talking to Cassie had enlivened her spirit. She didn't know who she should tell first. Should she tell everyone together, or tell Grandpa Charlie first and then tell her children? And when would she tell Baby Lena? She decided she would tell Charlie that night; she would pray about when to spread the news to the rest of the family. She hoped they would be as thrilled as she was. With everything going on, this could be either the best Christmas ever or the worst.

E. May smiled as she heard the voices of Baby Lena and Helene playing in the house. The two hadn't stopped running around since they got out of school for winter break. Santa Claus, presents, and candy were the only things on their minds. Both of them had been through so much in their short lives, yet they still had their joyful innocence. Unfortunately,

all that could be coming to an end. With that thought
E. May exhaled and said, "Lawd have mercy."

CHAPTER TWELVE

It was two days before Christmas, and Cassie was preparing for her trip home. She had convinced Kat to go with her and drive. She had decided to get a few presents for her parents, Baby Lena, and Kat. Her family didn't celebrate with a lot of gifts. The day was filled mostly with toys and presents for Baby Lena and Helene, lots of food and desserts, and plenty of laughter and music. Cassie beamed as she remembered the Christmas when she and Ray sang Marvin Gaye's "Ain't No Mountain High Enough." That spurred a family competition, with her father singing the Inkspot's "If I Didn't Care." He started off singing really high, and then when he got to the talking part his voice got really low. Normally E. May would have something to say about worldly music, but even she got a kick out of watching her family entertain themselves.

On the rare occasions her mother participated, she sang her favorite hymn "In Times Like These." Cassie closed her eyes, hearing her mother's strong voice. No matter when or where, she could be heard singing or humming that tune. And no matter what worldly songs the rest of them sang at Christmas, E. May was going to sing that song. The fond memories warmed Cassie's heart, and she knew in that instant she was ready to go home. Despite all that needed repairing within her family, she wanted to see them. She missed them, and she was okay admitting it. Yes, she felt betrayed. Yes, she felt used and unsupported. Yes, she had been mistreated, but she was ready to forgive. She needed to forgive. She needed to heal, and more importantly, she needed to prevent Baby Lena from enduring any further secrets and lies. Mother or not, she would do what was best for that child.

Ray had just finished hammering the last nail in the door when Aunt Peggie came and stood where he was. "Baby I sho' thank you for fixin' that ole door. You been a big help since you been here."

"No ma'am. It's the least I could do," Ray said. "For all you done, and not just for me but everybody. You always there."

"Baby I been blessed, and if you can't pass on the good that's been done to you, what good is it?"

"Yes ma'am," he answered. "Auntie, you thought any more about where you goin' for Christmas? I wish you would come with me to see yo' brother and the rest of the family."

"Would be nice, but you know that daughter of mine would have a fit if I didn't spend it with her and my grandbabies," she chuckled. "You know that means takin' my wallet."

"You know you gotta spoil yo' grandkids," he laughed.

"Yeah, but it's they mama and daddy who will have their hands out," she said. "So, where you gon' spend Christmas when you get there?"

"Auntie you know me. I gotta make my rounds. But I'ma make sure to see Baby Lena," he answered.

"Baby Lena. I remember like it was yesterday when Emma gave birth to that chile," she said, staring off. "She was the most beautiful baby I ever did see. Big bright eyes like she had been here before. She was a quiet li'l thing until she got mad. Boy, if she worked herself up it was hard to get her soothed. I remember, too, the look in Emma's eyes when she handed the baby over to Cassie. I ain't neva seen a hurt like that. Emma's heart broke up in a million tiny pieces that day. And to look at Cassie love on that chile like it was her own despite knowin' how she got here. I ain't neva seen nothin' like it. Cassie and Emma were always close growin' up.

"I probably shoulda said sumthin'. Maybe things would be different. Maybe that baby woulda left here in her real mama's arms."

Ray hadn't expected to hear any of that, and before he knew it there was a tear coming down his face. He wiped it away quickly with the back of his hand as he pretended to cough. Not knowing how to respond, Ray managed to say, "You always been here for us."

"Yeah, we do the best we can," she said, still looking off.

That was the first time Ray had actually understood the impact of what he had done. He had betrayed Cassie. He had ruined Emma and Cassie's relationship, and he had helped to deceive his own child. The reality made his stomach nauseous. This is what E. May was talking about when she said it was time to set things right.

When his aunt went back in the house, Ray's mind shifted from Baby Lena to the reason he had left Mississippi in the first place. *What happened to the man I shot? Am I murderer? Is somebody looking for me? Is it even safe to go back?* He didn't know, but he decided the consequences were worth it to see his daughter. He would go, stick close to family, and leave after a few days. He thought about what Cassie would be doing for Christmas. *Who had she been spending her Christmases with? Had she met someone?*

Ever since they were kids, Cassie was always the one the boys liked. She and Emma looked a lot alike, but they couldn't have been more different. Cassie was smart, pretty, and quiet. She was the cheerleader and the class president. The girls wanted to be her friend, and the boys wanted to date her. Emma was anything but quiet. She liked to laugh loud and have a good time. She was popular for different reasons. She had a reputation with the boys, and the girls knew not to mess with her. Emma wasn't a bad student, but because she enjoyed a wilder side of life it was hard for her to focus on her studies. Both Cassie and Emma had hearts of gold because of how they were raised.

Ray began spending time with Cassie when he was on the basketball team. He wasn't tall, but he was fast and could shoot the ball from anywhere on the court. He and Cassie would always exchange glances during the games or at practices, until one day he decided to ask her to help him with his homework. For several weeks they met at lunch, and he pretended to need help with math, until one day Cassie called him on it. By this time Ray had seen a side of Cassie not available to everyone. She had a great sense of humor and a flirtatious playfulness that hid a mystery. He had fallen in love with her, and they began spending all their free time together. He knew he would marry her after graduation because she was unlike any girl he had ever dated. Ray never imagined he would betray her love and destroy their family.

Moving in with Cassie's family was probably the biggest mistake they could have made. Ray had initially been able to resist Emma's advances and suggestions, but he was attracted to her edge. At the time, everyone had jobs or reasons to be gone during the day except Emma, and because Ray worked nights it was easy for them to find moments alone. The first time they slept together was supposed to be their last, but it became difficult because they traveled in the same circles. It was obvious to their friends that something was going on, but no one said anything to either of them. And no one knew they had already crossed the line. By the time Ray's conscience had caught up with him, Emma was already pregnant.

Ray could still see the look of shock and sadness in Cassie's face when he told her that Emma was pregnant with his child. The news sent the whole house into chaos, and all anyone could think about was how to keep the information from spilling out into the streets. The shame that the affair, Emma's illegitimate child, and the deception between sisters would bring was too much to comprehend.

The screaming and the yelling: Cassie and Emma, E. May and Emma, Ray and Emma, Cassie and Ray. It wasn't until Charlie spoke up and said enough. He said he would not have that continued commotion under his roof. So, for a month the quarrels were replaced by a tense silence, until one day Charlie and E. May called the three of them into the kitchen and told them Cassie and Emma would be going to Memphis to stay with their Aunt Peggie until the baby was born. If Ray and Cassie were to remain in the home, Ray and Emma must ask God's forgiveness and must never ever mess around again. There was no discussion. Ray wanted to go to Memphis too, but he was in no position to argue so he kept quiet and went along with the plan. The next day the sisters were taken to the train station.

Ray missed Cassie. He missed the calm that she brought to his life. Though he felt undeserving, he missed the genuine love she gave.

As Cassie finished packing for her trip, she thought about Ace. She needed to let him know for sure they weren't going to be able to spend Christmas together. She didn't know that he had already decided to go back to Chicago. The operations in Mississippi were in good hands, and he felt he needed to see Double T face to face to ensure him everything was under control. He had made arrangements for one of his boys to ride with him, and they were going to leave sometime before daylight, about 2:00 or 3:00 a.m. He didn't call Cassie; he knew she would call him if and when she was ready.

"Hello," Ace said cautiously.

"Merry Christmas, handsome!" Cassie said on the other end.

"Merry Christmas, baby," he said.

"Ace, I guess you know by now I'm not gon' be able to spend the holiday with you. My family and I ain't been gettin' along, and it wouldn't be right to bring you into all that."

"Baby, it's cool. I got business to tend to in Chicago, so I'll be leavin' town in the mornin'."

"Please be careful. I hear that Chicago weather ain't nothin' to mess with," she said somewhat surprised but also relieved. "Look Ace, I don't know what's gon' happen when I get back home, but I need you to know that should we lose contact, I'm okay. I really do care about you. Spendin' time with you over these past four months has opened me up to emotions I had forgotten were possible. Please know that."

Not knowing how to respond, Ace said, "Baby, you don't have to explain. You know how to find me."

"Thank you," she said. "Ace, please be safe. And have a Merry Christmas."

"I will pretty lady. You too," he said.

CHAPTER THIRTEEN

The ride to Pinola was quiet that Christmas morning. Cassie was preoccupied with thoughts about her family and Ace, not sure what she was facing or what she had potentially given up. Kat was focused on her father and the last Christmas they had spent together before he got sick and passed away. Nat King Cole could be heard on the radio, but neither of them was feeling very merry.

"We're two sad cases on this blessed Christmas mornin'," said Kat, breaking the silence in laughter. "I know what my issue is, but what the hell is goin' on with you? Wait, I know it's a tall, dark, and handsome-sized problem."

"Girl, where you get that from?" Cassie laughed. "You say the craziest sh-t. I swear."

"Chile, you and that man been dancin' around each other for months, and ain't neither one of you ready to tell the other what's really goin' on," she said. "You got secrets; he got secrets. All God's chillen got secrets!"

"What?!" Cassie said. "There ain't no problem. Ace and I have an understanding. We just talked a couple of days ago."

"Yeah, but I see you didn't deny there were secrets," Kat said, poking Cassie in the arm. "Look sis, I know you tryna' figure out what's gon' happen when you get home. All I can say is, think about that baby girl and let the truth be your guide."

Kat's words filled the car with silence once more, and all that could be heard was Eartha Kitt singing "Santa Baby."

Cassie envisioned Baby Lena. She was four years old the last time Cassie saw her. Baby Lena had always been wise beyond her years, and Cassie could only imagine how the girl would respond to finding out Emma was her real mother. The more she thought about it, the more she began to question why this news needed to be announced at all. But she couldn't explain her absence without divulging the truth of why she left in the first place.

Miles away at the Smith home, the atmosphere was a little more celebratory. The smell of baked cakes and pies, along with the pot of boiling mustard and turnip greens on the stove, floated through the air. Baby Lena and Helene were preoccupied on the floor with their new toys. Both got clothes, baby dolls, jacks, crayons, books, and a bag of penny candy. The hit of the morning was the blue baking oven they each had gotten. The family had contemplated getting one oven for the girls to share but realized it was best if each girl had her own. Grandpa Charlie had the turntable playing Christmas music. James Brown was singing "Santa Claus, Go Straight to the Ghetto." Emma, Johnny, and Freddy were drinking coffee and talking among themselves. E. May worked alone in the kitchen, putting the finishing touches on her dressing and potato salad. She hummed a happy tune as she put the dressing in the oven and drained the water off the potatoes.

She was delighted her eldest daughter was coming home. She had prayed the night before for peace and reconciliation, so she was confident the Lord would work it all out.

As Kat made the turn off the highway, the silence in the car seemed to get even louder.

"Baby Lena needs to know who her real mother is," Cassie said out of nowhere. "She needs to know that if I were her real mother, I neva would have abandoned her. She needs to know she's loved, and that we grown folks can make some bad decisions sometimes that can really hurt people, even the people we love."

Kat didn't attempt to respond. She knew that it was a private conversation between Cassie and herself.

"She needs to know that we made some bad choices, but that the love for her is very real. There will neva be a good time to tell her, so we can't let her grow up not knowin' the truth. Every child has a right to know who their mama and daddy is. No one has the right to keep that secret, no matter how ugly the truth is." Cassie sighed. "I don't know how it's gon' be once she realizes I'm her aunt and not her mama.

"This is not my fault." Cassie was becoming emotional. "I didn't sleep around on my husband. I'm a victim too."

With those words the ultimate cause of Cassie's separation from her family had finally surfaced for her. All the pain she had hidden, all the hurt she had revisited every year on Baby Lena's birthday, was present in that statement. Cassie may have sounded unhappy, but inside her heart and spirit were healing from years of brokenness. She felt freer than she had been in years. The truth of her words was liberating. She had nothing to be ashamed of, and she was determined to go home with her head held high. She was grateful that this revelation had come when it did and grateful that the family was able to gather to begin its own healing.

"Thank you, Kat," Cassie said, turning to her friend. "You been a real friend. I wouldn't be here if it weren't for you: the job, the talks, the laughs, the friendship, the sisterhood. Girl, you just don't know.

"Today is Christmas, and I'm gettin' my life back. Merry Christmas, Katrina," she smiled.

"Merry Christmas, Cassie." Kat remained focused on the road. She felt the same about Cassie, and one day she would tell her.

As they got closer to the house, Kat turned off the main street onto a narrow gravel road.

Her family's home was the largest one in the neighborhood because it was once owned by a prominent White family that her grandfather, father, and uncles had all worked for. When the patriarch of that family died, his children sold the house to Cassie's father. The rumor was that her dad paid $1.00 for the house just so it couldn't be said the house was given to him. Once Cassie's family moved in, it didn't take long for the other White families to start moving out.

At the end of the road Cassie could see the house and the cars in the front. As they pulled up closer, three German Shepherds came from around back to greet them.

"Just pull over there," Cassie pointed. "Hey King. Hey Buddy. Hey Queenie."

Kat parked the car and turned off the ignition. "You ready?" She looked at Cassie.

"Let's do it." Cassie exhaled and opened the door to greet the excited dogs. "Hey y'all," she said, bending down to quickly pet each one before shooing them away.

"Who there?" said Charlie, straining to see from the porch.

"Merry Christmas, Daddy," she hollered.

"What—Cassie? Girl!" Charlie walked off the porch with a delight and energy he seldom displayed.

"Merry Christmas, Daddy. I'm your gift," she grinned.

"I'll say. This sho' is a gift," he said, hugging his daughter. "Yo' mama said you was comin'!"

"Yes sir. I'm here."

"Well, come on in the house." He extended his hand to Kat. "Young lady, I'm Charles Smith."

"Daddy, this my good friend Katrina."

"Alright, pleasure to meet you. Y'all come on inside." Charlie grabbed their suitcases.

By this time Johnny, Freddy and Emma were standing on the porch. Seeing their smiling faces Cassie knew she was where she belonged. She was home. "Merry Christmas, y'all!" she shouted.

"Merry Christmas, li'l sister!" said Johnny.

"Girl, it's good to see ya'," said Freddy.

Cassie hugged both of her brothers. When she saw her sister, the two reluctantly reached for each before embracing.

"Merry Christmas, Cassie," Emma said with a shaky voice. "Glad you home."

"Merry Christmas," Cassie said. "I'm glad to be home."

By now the news of Cassie's arrival had spread to Baby Lena, Helene, and E. May.

"Mommy! Mommy! Mommy!" was all that Cassie could hear. Making her way through the crowd was Baby Lena. "Mommy! You came for Christmas!"

"Merry Christmas, baby girl," Cassie said, picking up the child and squeezing her tight. "I missed you, little one."

"I missed you too, Mommy." Baby Lena took her tiny hand and rubbed her mother's face.

Standing in the background was E. May. She had begun to cry. Her family was together again. Despite the ugliness and pain they had been through, despite the secrets they had yet to disclose, her family was reunited.

Cassie held Baby Lena, kissing her cheeks and patting her back. The little girl smelled of syrup and hair grease as she held her close. Cassie didn't want to let go. Yet, seeing Baby Lena's innocent face reminded her of the lie she must expose. It was a bittersweet reunion. Cassie was prepared to tell her the truth, but she was not prepared to say goodbye to the baby she had raised as her own. Even if it all had been a lie, the love she had for Baby Lena was honest and true.

"Let me give your grandma a hug," Cassie said, putting Baby Lena down.

"Merry Christmas, Mama," she said.

"Merry Christmas, Cass." E. May stretched out her arms.

Cassie rested in her mother's hug just as Baby Lena had done to her.

"My baby home," E. May cried. "Thank you Lawd. All my babies home."

"I missed you, Mama," Cassie said. "I'm glad to be home. I really am."

"Alright, that's enough of that," Charlie rang out. "Let them girls get settled. Cassie, introduce yo' friend to the family."

Kat stood in the background with Cassie's siblings. After the introductions everyone found their place throughout the house. Charlie put a new album on the record player, and the voices of everyone talking brought the noise level up in each room. Cassie, Kat, and Emma sat around the kitchen table while E. May finished dinner. Baby Lena and Helene took turns showing Cassie what they got for Christmas, with Baby Lena stopping frequently to sit in her mother's lap.

Cassie caught Emma's glances a few times and noticed something she had not seen before. Surprisingly, it was the look of shame and regret. *Had Emma experienced her own revelation? Had she finally realized the consequences of her actions?*

As if no time had passed, the conversation between the women flowed from the latest news about the family to general news and gossip circulating throughout the community.

"Mama, tell 'em about the man they found dead at the bus station," Emma said.

"Chile, I don't wanna talk about nothin' like that on Christmas," E. May said. "Sho' is sad though to die and don't nobody know ya'."

It was after 1:00 p.m. when Ray arrived in Mississippi. His cousin picked him up from the station and drove him to his aunt's house, where everyone was gathering for the holiday. He hadn't seen his Aunt Gee since that night everything happened.

Walking into the small shotgun house, Ray felt comfort and relief. He went through greeting his aunts, uncles, cousins, and family friends, who were all crowded into the small space. His Aunt Gee, as well as some of the other elders, were in the kitchen.

"Merry Christmas, y'all!" he said joyfully. "Auntie Gee, you lookin' mighty foxy!"

"You don't look half bad yo'self," she joked back. The two embraced as everyone laughed at their playfulness.

"Boy, you been by to see yo' baby?" asked one of his uncles.

"No sir, not yet. I'll be headin' that way later."

"Damn shame. That chile growin' up with her maw in one place and her paw in another." The old man shook his head in disgust as he spit tobacco in a soda can.

"Yes sir," was all Ray said. He thought how ironic and unfair it was that Cassie was being judged for leaving *her* child.

CHAPTER FOURTEEN

Dinner felt like old times with everyone around the table: Charlie, E. May, Freddy, Johnny, Cassie, Emma, Kat, Baby Lena, and Helene. E. May had every dish prepared to perfection. The aromas of sliced ham, turkey, dressing, macaroni and cheese, sweet potato pie, greens, potato salad, cornbread, and cranberry sauce filled the whole house with a single fragrance of warmth and cheer.

The conversation and laughter flowed freely as everyone ate as much as they wanted. Neither Cassie nor Emma thought about the conversation that was to come later. Baby Lena and Helene were in a world of their own, having their own private discussion. Every now and then Baby Lena would lay her head on Cassie's arm, and Cassie would exchange the affection by randomly hugging her or kissing the top of her head.

A few times Charlie and E. May shot each other knowing looks. They were relieved to have their children together under one roof. While all this was going on, Freddy and Kat had realized their mutual attraction and were talking privately.

"Cassie, you and Kat stayin' the night, ain't you?" her mother asked.

"Yes ma'am. That's what we planned," she answered.

Knock. Knock. Knock. "Merry Christmas, Smith family!" someone called from the front porch. It was Ray. He had prolonged the visit as long as he could, arriving close to five o'clock.

"It's my daddy!" Baby Lena said, jumping out of her seat. "Merry Christmas, Daddy!" she yelled as she ran to the door.

Ray came in carrying several gifts. "All those mine?" Baby Lena stretched her arms trying to reach the packages.

"Most of 'em." Ray put the gifts down and grabbed his daughter in his arms. "Merry Christmas, everybody." He looked around the table. His heart skipped a beat when he noticed Cassie, but he maintained his composure and continued to talk to Baby Lena.

"Daddy, guess who's here!" she said, hugging Ray. "Mommy! Mommy's here!"

"She is?" he said. "Well, that's alright!" Walking over to the table, Ray acknowledged everyone. When he got to Cassie, he wanted to tell her how sorry he was and how beautiful she looked, but all he said was, "Cassie, glad you back. You look good, girl."

"Good to see you too." She hadn't thought about how it would feel to see Ray again. Surprisingly, she didn't have any strong feelings – positive or negative. She held no animosity for his betrayal, and she felt no urge to recapture what they once had.

"Ray, come around here and get you a plate," E. May said. "The food taste pretty good, if I say so myself." The comment made everyone laugh.

"May, you know this boy gon' eat," Charlie interjected. "He ain't neva turned down a meal."

"Yes sir," said Ray. "I may be crazy, but I ain't no fool. Mama E. May cook, I'm eatin' sumthin'." Ray put Baby Lena down so he could wash his hands and get a plate. He had already eaten at his aunt's house. The food there was good, but it wasn't the same. As he fixed his plate from the dishes on the table, Baby Lena said, "Daddy, you can sit in my chair."

"Thank you, baby," he said. Baby Lena sat in her mother's lap and smiled as she watched her father eat. *Mommy and Daddy are together just like I wished for.*

Cassie held Baby Lena as she too watched Ray eat. Inside she grieved all the times like these the three of them missed and would never have. That was the last time their family would be a family. The fact made her feel a deep sense of loss. She hugged Baby Lena a little tighter.

By the time Ray finished his meal, E. May had cut slices of her desserts and set them on the table. Charlie had turned on the record player, and The Jackson 5's "I Saw Mommy Kissing Santa Claus" was playing in the background. Freddy and Kat had gone outside so they could smoke. Johnny was letting Helene teach him how to play jacks. Emma, feeling uncomfortable, had left the room. She was unusually quiet, and everyone noticed.

"Y'all come get some of this cake and pie," E. May said as she made a plate for herself.

One by one everyone came to the table. Freddy and Kat got their plates and quickly returned outside to be alone. Baby Lena took advantage of the opportunity to eat from Cassie's plate. Ray caught glimpses of his wife and daughter and smiled. He shocked them both when he took the last morsel of pound cake from Cassie's plate. His antics caused them to giggle.

"Li'l girl, you gon' be a stuffed tick goin' to bed tonight," Cassie said, rubbing Baby Lena's stomach.

"All of us are," said E. May. "Thank the good Lawd we don't eat like this but twice a year."

"Whatchu talkin''bout May?" Charlie chimed in. "We eat like this Christmas, Thanksgiving, Easter, Mother's Day, Father's Day, and every Sunday."

The comment brought laughter to the room. "You sho' right about it!" E. May said.

As the evening went along, Charlie changed up the music and began playing Jerry Butler's "I Stand Accused."

"It's 'bout time for those girls to get ready for bed," E. May said.

"Okay Mama. I'ma put Baby Lena to bed in a li'l bit," said Cassie.

"You wanna take a walk outside with me?" Cassie whispered to Baby Lena.

"Uh-huh," the girl said, nodding.

Everyone, as if rehearsed, seemed to stop talking when the two got up from the table.

"You want me to come too?" Ray asked.

"Can Daddy come too?" Baby Lena asked.

"Not right now," Cassie answered. "This is our special time."

The two walked outside and stepped off the porch to head over to the swing.

"Come on and sit next me," she said to Baby Lena. "Did you have a good Christmas?"

"Yes, it was my favorite Christmas ever," Baby Lena beamed with joy. "You came home. Daddy is here, and nobody is getting mad."

"Yeah, I'm glad nobody got mad too," Cassie said. "Baby Lena, I'm sorry I stayed gone for so long.

"There's a lot that I need to tell you, and it may be hard for you to understand. But no matter what you hear, remember one thing: You are loved, and God created you so special.

"Do you understand?" she asked.

"Yes ma'am," Baby Lena responded innocently.

"Grown-ups are older than children, but that don't mean we always do what's right," Cassie said. "And because we are older, when we do something wrong a lot of people can get hurt. But God is so big and powerful, He can bring something good out of something bad.

"Do you understand?" she asked again.

"Yes ma'am," Baby Lena answered.

"Seven years ago something happened, and instead of telling the truth, we as a family made a mistake by telling a lie about where you came from.

"Your Aunt Emma and I went to Memphis, and that's where you were born. Only, you didn't come from my stomach. You came from your Aunt Emma's stomach." Cassie took deep breath.

"Baby Lena, your Aunt Emma is your real mama, and I am your aunt. You understand?"

"You not my mama because I came from my Aunt Emma's stomach and not your stomach," Baby Lena recited back. "My daddy is still my daddy."

"Yea. That's it, baby girl. How you feel about that?" Cassie looked at Baby Lena, waiting for her response.

"Did you leave me because I didn't come from your stomach?" The little girl searched Cassie's face for an answer.

"No, no. I left because I wished you had come from my stomach," said Cassie surprised by the question. "I love you like you were my very own, and I always will. You didn't come from my stomach, but you live in my heart." Cassie took Baby Lena's hand and placed it on her chest.

"It hurt me to know that we were hiding the truth from you. I was hurt by a lot of other things too, but it was neva about my love for you.

"I'm sorry I left you, and I hope you can forgive me. I hope you will forgive all of us for the mistakes we made and for not tellin' you the truth.

"Baby Lena, we all want what's best for you, and that's to know who you are and where you came from.

"If you mad or upset, that's okay. If you got questions, that's okay too," Cassie said, trying to read Baby Lena's face. "Just make sure you talk to somebody: me, your mama Emma, your daddy, your Grandma E. May—somebody. Don't ever hold your feelins' inside.

"And just like you and I are talkin' now, your mama Emma is gonna wanna have her say, and your daddy is gonna wanna have his say.

"You may not be able to understand all this now, but as you get older, you will. And how you feel about all this may change. You might be sad or mad. There may come a time when you don't know how you feel. And you know what? All that's okay, cuz your family is here. We gon' always be here, and we'll answer any questions you have."

Baby Lena's little mind was racing. She thought back to her birthday party and the fights between her Aunt Emma and her daddy. She wondered if that was why they didn't like each other. She also wondered if her mother and Aunt Emma could be friends again. "Do I have to call you Aunt Cassie now and Aunt Emma mama?"

"What do you want to call me?" Cassie answered.

"Can I still call you mama for a little while longer?" she replied.

"That's fine with me, but we need to talk to your mama Emma too. Is that okay?"

"Yeah, that's okay," Baby Lena replied. "Mama?"

"Yeah?" Cassie answered through her tears.

"I'm sorry I didn't come from your stomach," Baby Lena said, getting into her lap.

"I am too, li'l girl. I am too."

The two sat quietly swinging in the coolness of the night, each holding onto that moment and each other.

AN INSPIRATIONAL WORD:
LIVING FREE

And ye shall know the truth, and the truth shall make you free. John 8:32 KJV

In the Bible, Jesus explains to his disciples who He is and what His purpose is as the revelation of God to humanity. Jesus tells them that their acceptance of Him, their faith in Him, will bring them freedom from the power and penalty of sin. Thus, living an abundant life with the promise of an eternal future as explained in John 3:16.

We are currently living in a society that doesn't always value the truth. From the most prominent figures to the most private citizens, the truth is often looked at as an option rather than a responsibility. While a lie can seem like a convenient resolution to a problem or a situation, its consequences are often more costly and entangling than the problem the lie was meant to help resolve.

Are the consequences worth it? This is the question you must ask yourself. Some people may answer yes. Others may regret the restrictions and limitations their lie has placed on their life. When we give space to lies, we imprison ourselves with guilt, shame, bitterness, anger or unforgiveness, all the negative by-products of a life that is not free. The result can be destructive behavior to oneself or others. The saying is true "hurt people do hurt people."

Truth is a superpower; it makes you free. Free to forgive. Free to heal. Free to grow. Free to move forward. Free to move on. The truth frees you from what has you bound and liberates you to receive all that is possible: forgiveness, restoration, transformation, maturation, elevation and redemption. Why live entangled when Christ came to set you free?

Is there a lie that has you confined? Break free with the truth. Admit and acknowledge what is real and true about yourself, others, and the situation you are in. Life is worth living unconstrained. Accept truth, speak truth, live truth, and be free.

A PRAYER FOR LIVING FREE

God, the Father of all, I thank you for the freedom that comes from accepting and following your Word. In a world that doesn't always value the truth, give me courage to stand in truth, live in truth, speak truth, and be free. Forgive me if a lie I have told has caused me or someone else to be entangled by its deception. Lord, release me from any hurt or betrayal that may be hindering my progress. And Lord, as you forgive my trespasses, please forgive those who have trespassed against me.

My life is worth living unconstrained. From this moment on, I choose to live free in your Word. My heart, my mind, my body, and my soul, through your spirit of forgiveness, are now free. In the name of Jesus, I receive it and thank you for it. Amen.

CPSIA information can be obtained
at www.ICGtesting.com
Printed in the USA
LVHW020057120523
746592LV00010B/407